THE
SINGING
CAT

THE
SINGING CAVE

EILÍS DILLON

POOLBEG

First published 1959 by
Faber and Faber, London
This paperback edition published 1991 by
Poolbeg Press Ltd Knocksedan House,
Swords, Co Dublin, Ireland
Reprinted 1992

Poolbeg Press receives financial assistance from
The Arts Council / An Chomhairle Ealaíon, Ireland.

ISBN 1 85371 211 6

Cover design by Carol Betera
Set by Richard Parfrey
Printed by Cox & Wyman Ltd Reading Berks

Contents

1

I Discover the Singing Cave

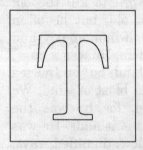

he night before I discovered the Singing Cave brought the worst storm I have ever seen in our part of Connemara. It began in the afternoon. Before dark, every west-facing door in the island was firmly shut and covered on the inside with a heavy straw mat to keep out the draughts.

In my grandfather's house the people came visiting as usual, but their talk was uneasy. It was all about shifting boats to safety, and whether the thatch of the houses would hold firm, and how the wind had whipped away the bladderwrack that had been left to drip on the walls. We did not mind this much, for we knew there would be a great harvest of weed lying on the foreshore when the storm would be over.

1

"'Tis the days of the Old Cow, of course," said Lord Folan. "We can expect storms always at this time."

The old men used to say that March borrowed three days from April to kill the old cow. Lord Folan was not old, but he often repeated these sayings half-humorously and almost as if he believed them. He was a huge, slow-moving man on dry land, but on the sea in a currach he was like a blast of wind. We were very proud of him, for he was the champion oarsman of all the islands. He was nicknamed Lord for his slow, dignified ways.

Our island is Barrinish. It is the last of a chain of four that stretches out into the Atlantic Ocean between Clifden Bay and Golam Head. They are linked to each other and to the mainland by bridges, which are sometimes convenient for taking a load of turf or a herd of bullocks in to Galway. But even for these purposes we prefer to use hookers when the weather is fair. Barrinish is shaped like a crescent moon. Most of the houses are on its inner curve, which is called Norseman's Bay.

My grandfather and I lived alone at this time. His house was a little west of the village, beautifully placed at a turn of the road under the shelter of a little hill. It looked down on a deep blue lake, ringed with reeds, in which our ducks loved to paddle. Beyond the house, the land stretched away upwards to tall cliffs that dropped sheer into the Atlantic Ocean. We grazed our sheep there in good weather, but it was too cold and sandy for crops.

On Brosna, which is the next island, my father and mother, my uncle and my two older brothers lived together in our house. Though my father owned four holdings of land, there was not enough work for so many men. This was why my mother had thought of apprenticing me to the tailor in Barrinish.

When my grandfather heard about it, he flew into a rage. He thumped up and down our kitchen waving his arms and shouting:

"Is he never to go to the bog, never to go out in a boat, never to cut a field of barley, never to sow a ridge of spuds? Is he to sit all day on a table, like a china dog on the mantelpiece? That's no life for a man!"

"But his hands would never be dirty," said my poor mother. I could see she was wishing now that she had never thought of this plan.

"And tell me now, how could you trust a man whose hands are never dirty?" the old man demanded. "If you don't want that boy, you can give him to me. I'll know how to treat him. I won't put him fiddly-fiddling with little bitty-bits of cloth till he's blind as a bat and cranky as an old maid. You give that boy to me, I say!"

So they did, partly to stop him from stumping up and down the kitchen, frightening the cat and raising the dust and shouting loud enough to be heard over in the Aran Islands.

You may be sure I was pleased at this. The tailor in Barrinish had a crooked leg which he curled up under him, comfortably enough, when he sat cross-legged on the table to sew. But I was convinced that his leg was in this state from continually sitting on it, and I had been miserable for a week at the thought of becoming like him.

So now I felt like a reprieved prisoner. My grandfather and I had a fine life together. Though he was so much older than me, he was always as ready for fun as I was myself. We went fishing and hunting seals all along the coast. We watched out for the foreign ships coming into the Bay and rowed out to meet them in the currach. Several times, when they were leaving, we had sailed off after them in our hooker, and had spent some wonderful days at old Breton and Spanish port towns, where the trawlers and lobster-boats came from. And in the rest of the time I helped him to farm his land and mind his sheep and cattle. In return for this he gave me sixpence every week, and he had promised to leave me the farm in his will. I was quite content with my bargain.

We were never short of company. The men came to us in the evenings because the fire was always good, the talk was always interesting, and there was no woman to look at the clock while the night was still young and say: "Now, men, it's time to be going home." And it was a pleasant little walk from the village, not too far after a hard day's work.

On the night of the storm, we built up a fine fire as if it had still been winter, and settled down for a long gossip. I remember that Rooster Hernon was there, with his red hair standing up higher and wilder than usual. It had been blown about, I suppose, by the wind outside. He sat close by me, as far as possible from Lord Folan. Rooster was a good man in a currach too, but he was not as good as Lord, being looser jointed. He was never satisfied with his inferiority. He seemed to feel that hatred for Lord would give him extra energy for the oars when the currach races were on. I have always thought that this was wrong, and that he only wasted his wind just at the time when he needed it most. Now he whispered venomously into my ear, glaring across the little circle at Lord:

"Look at him, the big fellow! Look at the way he sits, like the Queen of Sheba! Wouldn't it turn a horse from his oats, the pride of him—"

"Ah, now, Rooster, don't be so hard on him," said I soothingly. "He's not proud."

My heart was in my mouth lest Lord might hear and take offence. There were drawbacks to the honour of having the visiting house. Rooster was still grumbling under his breath. My grandfather heard him and came across at once to relieve me of my burden.

"Run outside, Pat, and see if the bullocks are safe," he said.

I went thankfully. As I opened the back door so that the wind went whistling around the kitchen, I heard Rooster's voice raised derisively:

"Ha, Lordeen! You wouldn't do much good in your currach tonight!"

"'Tis true for you, Rooster," said Lord calmly.

I wondered as I had often done before whether Rooster would have been so bold if

Lord Folan's temper had been as short as his own.

Outside, I had sheltered until I came to the corner of the house. There must have been a moon somewhere high among the heavy, racing clouds, for I could see when I turned the corner how the wallflowers were all lying flat on the ground, and the two green balls of glass, with which I had decorated the front step, had been hurled across the yard and were smashed to pieces. I avoided the splinters for the sake of my bare toes and crossed the road to look into the bullocks' field.

I leaned on the wall to count their black shapes. The wind roared and whistled around me so that I thought I would be rolled to the ground, but the bullocks lay about the field as steady as growing rocks, chewing their silly cud as calmly as if it had been a summer evening. Only one was over by the newly walled-up gap, nosing at the stones to knock them down. I knew that bullock well. He hated to be confined in a field or a shed and he always went to the trouble of opening up a way out for himself. When he had done this, he often stayed in the next field or even wandered in and out through the gap he had made.

Still, tonight I did not trust him. I went down to the gap and replaced the stones that he had knocked. Then I turned him back into the field about his business.

Even in the few minutes since I had left the house, the wind had risen. I had to fight every foot of my way back. When I came into the warm kitchen again, old Luke Duffy, sitting on the creepy stool as near to the fire as it was safe to go, was thumping his stick in the ashes so that they flew up and made everyone cough. All the men fell silent, for they knew he would not stop thumping until they did.

" 'Tis foreshown to me," said Luke in his high, cracked whining voice, "that the wind won't stop rising this night until it begins to rain!"

He looked around triumphantly at the company. No one laughed. Lord Folan gave a wise nod, as if he had just heard an important piece of news. Luke thumped again, but only once. The men began to chat among themselves, for that last thump was the signal that the old man had finished speaking for a while.

It was no more than eleven o'clock when they got up to go. Lord Folan was the first to move.

"I'll just walk up and see how Johnny Gill's house is standing against the wind," he said.

Mattie Connor, the blacksmith, said he would go with him. He was as big as Lord and as slow of speech, but because he owned no land and wore an apron at his work, he was not treated with such respect. Mattie, being a businessman, had money in the bank, but no one cared a fig for that. Corny Lynch, who owned the shop in the village, was spoken of with the same careless pity, though he could buy and sell every man in the parish. I suppose it's hard to respect a man in an apron.

Mattie Connor and Lord Folan were alike in more ways than showed at first sight. It was no surprise to any of us that it was they who thought of visiting Johnny Gill before going home. When Lord's own work was done, he was usually to be found digging a neighbour's field, or mending someone's boat, or making a fishing-line for a child. And Mattie was always ready with an excuse for repairing a gate free of charge, or shoeing a poor widow's donkey at half-price.

Visiting Johnny Gill was a greater charity than any of these. He lived alone in a little one-roomed cottage just under the ridge of the island.

The only way to his house was by a quaking grass-grown track which had been the old road over the mountain. If you succeeded in reaching Johnny's door, you might find it shut against you in spite of all your knocking, while Johnny skipped about inside and laughed to himself at your discomfiture. He had a great secret source of information about the people of Barrinish, he said. On the long, lonely nights, while he sat over his ashy fire, he could hear the water talking in the kettle, telling him fearful things about the neighbours' doings. He liked both Lord and the blacksmith, however, so it was thought that he would let them into the house to make sure that he would be safe for the night.

When the last man had gone out, I covered the fire with ashes while my grandfather slowly wound the big sallow-faced wall clock.

"I like to see people come, and I like to see them go," he said to me with a grin.

When he had lit a candle for each of us and had blown out the oil lamp, we stood for a moment in the middle of the kitchen and listened to the thundering of the sea and the wind. It was a doleful sound. It seemed to me that the house shook a little. My grandfather said:

"Would you like to sleep in my room tonight, Patcheen?"

"I'll be all right, thanks," I said coolly, though I guessed that seven hobgoblins were lurking at this very moment under my bed.

He did not press me, but I knew that I was free to change my mind. On many a stormy night after a similar lofty refusal, I had had to light my candle and skip across the kitchen from my own room to the old man's, and share his vast bed.

Tonight, however, I stood my ground. I rolled my ears in my feather-bed so as to reduce the horrid noise, and presently I drifted into sleep.

I slept heavily, as one must in a feather-bed, and I was mighty relieved when I awoke to find pale daylight at the window. The sky was as white as milk. The rain had not started yet, and the wind still groaned and shrieked even louder than it had done last night. I thought of that contrary bullock and wondered if he had been content to stay with the others. Once I had thought of him, I could sleep no more.

The cold flagstones of the floor stung my feet so that I hopped from foot to foot while I was dressing. My door creaked as I opened it gently but I knew that my grandfather could not have heard it above the bellowing of the wind. I paused in the kitchen to lay a few sods of turf on the ashes of the fire, so that they would light easily on my return. Then I slipped out through the back door and around the corner of the house.

Immediately I felt as if I were gripped in a pair of giant arms that were trying to lift me off the ground. The air was full of strange, wild scents and tastes that seemed to have been carried on it from faraway places and mixed delightfully with our own homely smells of salt and seaweed and turf-smoke and spring grass. Away down below me, the thundering sea was a greenish-grey edged with white. Farther west, where the cliffs were, the spray from the tall waves moved in a cloud over the land. Some of it even sprinkled my face where I stood.

Then I saw our bullock. He was standing on a rocky spur of the cliff, that overhung the sea. He was stock still, with his head down and his legs splayed out as if to steady himself against the force of the wind which every moment struggled to send him plunging down between the spur and the cliff's face. I remembered my grandfather's exasperated words, that one day that bullock's adventurous spirit would be the death of him. For a moment I thought of leaving him to his fate, but then I could not find it in my heart to abandon him.

To get to the cliff-top, I had to cross three walled fields and climb a long unsheltered slope covered with short sour grass. The wind beat around my ears. Walking against it was like trying to get through a wall of glass. As I climbed higher, every step became more difficult, and soon I was drenched and blinded with spray. No doubt it was the same spray which had washed away the last of the bullock's feeble wits.

Long before I reached him, I was down on my hands and knees. With my heart in my mouth, I crawled out on to the spur of rock. A moment later I had him by the tail.

It was while I was hauling at him that the cave below began to sing. It was a long, deep, ringing sound, as I have often imagined the bells of drowned ships must ring under a swelling sea. It filled me with instant terror, for all in a flash I imagined that the spur of rock had broken off under the combined weight of myself and the bullock and that the sound

I heard was the triumphant sea's hungry song.

Even when this fancy had left me, still I was shaken with strange fears. The sound ebbed and flowed now with every gust of wind, and reminded me of descriptions I had been given of the banshee's wail, which is only heard when someone is going to die.

Then all at once I remembered that the cave just under this part of the cliff was always called the Singing Cave. It was a shallow niche in the cliff's face, hardly worth visiting though I had been there once or twice in my currach. It could only be approached from the sea. Usually the waves moved in and out of it with a sluggish, dead sound. Because of a sudden shelving of the rock it was dry at low water, but when the tide was full the sea just covered its floor.

There were many stories about the reason for its name. Some people said that the seals always swam in there and sang before a storm, so that the fishermen out in their boats would hear them and come home to safety. There was sense in this story if you believed, as most of my neighbours did, that seals are inhabited by the souls of drowned sailors. Certainly their round melancholy eyes and drooping moustaches have a very human look about them. Another story was that a local man, on the run from the soldiers with his wife, had hidden her in the cave for safety. But he was killed and the tide had come up and drowned her though she sang and sang in the hope that someone would hear and come to her rescue. So, they say, still she sings at every spring tide. But I had never met anyone who had himself heard singing in this place. Though my head was full of these stories, I did not loose my hold on the bullock's tail. I heaved as if I were hoisting the sail of a hooker. At first this only made him plant his feet more firmly on the ground, but presently he took a step backwards and then I knew that I had the better of him. Little by little I backed him down off the cliff. As I went, the singing grew fainter with every step. By the time I had reached the lane beyond our house, to a stranger it would have been no more than a whistling of the wind.

Still I knew that if one of the neighbours happened to have a reason for walking out towards the cliff, the strange, wild sound would become the talk of the island. The boats would be out, clustered like puffins around the mouth of the cave. I would be brushed aside with all the other boys. I might even be left behind, if my grandfather's currach filled up too quickly with boatless neighbours. That had happened when the drifting whale was sighted, only last autumn. I had not been very much put out about the whale. His smell had been carried to us powerfully on the beach, so that I quickly lost my wish to see him closer. But by now my curiosity to visit the Singing Cave was so strong that I would almost have put out in a currach there and then, on that terrible sea.

Of course, this was impossible. I knew that I would not even have crested the first wave. I brought the bullock back to the field where he belonged and gave him a lecture about his sins. He seemed to have learned a lesson at last, for he joined the herd meekly enough.

Back in the kitchen, my grandfather had the kettle on. I told him how I had just rescued the bullock. He laughed shortly.

"There's truth in the old saying that the day might come when the cow would need her tail," he said. "The sooner that bullock goes to market the better for us all. He can break someone else's heart then."

We made our breakfast, of strong red tea

and soda-bread and eggs. We always baked our own bread, and boasted that it was the best man-made bread in the island. While we ate I told my grandfather about the strange sound that I had heard on the cliff-top.

"It's the Singing Cave for sure," I said. "Something has happened there. We must go and see it the first minute that the wind drops."

My grandfather agreed to this at once. Naturally, he wanted to visit the cave before anyone else, for above all things he loved to be able to tell a piece of strange or terrible news.

Twenty times during the day he went to the door to see if the wind were slackening in force. When the neighbours came in at the fall of night he questioned them closely until he had discovered where each man had spent the day. When he found that they had all stayed near home, he was satisfied.

The men were full of talk about the destruction done by the storm but not one of them spoke of the Singing Cave. Like us, they had been busy at mending nets and harness and tools, and making furniture or painting. These things were always left for stormy days when it was impossible to work outside.

Some time during that night, the rain began, but it was two days before we were able to launch the currach and row to the cave.

2

The Viking

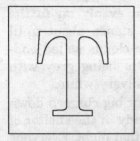hose two days were like
to kill me. I spent the
time in telling my
grandfather to have patience, and that we
could afford to wait. The wind had dropped a
great deal with the rain. I had been up on the
cliff-top, and I knew that the Cave was not
singing now. Down below me the sea swelled
wickedly, a dull, heavy green, with its surface
blown constantly by the wind so that I could
not see through it. I knew by its irregular
heaving motion that it would swallow a
currach in one restless bite. Even now the
waves struck the cliff's face so sharply that
thin fountains of spray shot into the air, high
enough for their wavering tips to look at me
where I stood.

By the evening of the second day, the rain

had stopped. Rabbits were scuttling in and out of their sandy burrows, larks sang wild and free in a hazy blue sky and turfs of sea-pink began to show suddenly against the green slope that led up to the cliff. The sea was dark blue, rolling in evenly on to the beach and dragging the stones about until they rattled. Great white clouds sailed endlessly above us. Instead of being grey with storm, their edges were silvery white.

Before dark, we took our big currach down to the shore and left it ready in the shelter of a rock. We had no visitors that night. Everyone was restoring order after the storm and preparing for the next day's work. I wished that we had had a full house, for it would have passed the evening much more quickly. As well as that, I would have liked to have had the men here where I could see them, for I was convinced by now that everyone was as anxious as I was to visit the cave.

In the morning, we found that the wind had moved a point to the south. The sea was shining under a sweet, gentle breeze, so that I was reminded of the peaceful innocence of a cross baby who has at last fallen asleep.

Through the open kitchen door the scent of wallflowers filled the room while we ate a hurried breakfast.

A steep path led from our house down to the sea. This morning it ran with water like a stream after the rain. The sky was high and clear, but the Aran Islands showed a greenish-grey so that we knew there was more rain coming.

We launched the currach, with a sharp eye out lest one of our neighbours might think we were going fishing and might offer to come along with us. We took a pair of oars each for speed. Soon we were shooting out between the long fingers of rock that formed our little harbour.

We kept as close under the cliffs as we dared, so as not to be seen. At this early hour, they cast a broad shadow, cold and mysterious. The mouth of the cave was a black patch on the grey limestone. The tide was falling, but there was still enough water within the cave to float the currach.

We shipped the oars a little distance out from the cliff and glided silently into the darkness, holding the cold cave walls with our hands so as not to be washed out again on the next wave.

"The candle," said my grandfather. "It will stay alight in here out of the breeze."

I fumbled about until I found it, and a box of matches. The little yellow flame was cheerful, as I held it high to light up the cave. It laid a long streak of yellow on the dead black water. Then my grandfather said, very quietly:

"Look at the back wall, Pat. There is the cause of the song you heard."

I turned to look.

It seemed as if a great organ had been erected in the cave. When I had been here before I had noticed that the back wall was ridged vertically from floor to ceiling, and each ridge was polished smooth by the continual stroking of the waves. Now every second ridge had fallen out, leaving long empty gaps through which the light air moved even now with a delicate humming sound. It was like an echo of the majestic, full-throated song that I had heard during the storm. And it was quite plain that beyond these stone organ-pipes there was another, deeper cave.

One of the gaps between the ridges was wider than the rest.

"I could fit through there," I said to my grandfather, pointing.

"You could, faith," said he.

We were silent while we thought about it. The candle flame flickered quietly. I did not want to creep through that narrow space. I think I had some faint notion that it might close up again as mysteriously as it had opened, and imprison me within. Still I knew that I could not tamely turn my back on it, and suffer my curiosity for the rest of my life.

"It's likely enough to be dry in there," I said at last, "unless there's a big drop inside."

I shivered a little at the thought of the big drop, possibly with a fat monster below, lying in wait to bite the legs off me.

"If there was a drop, we'd hear the water sucking in and out of it," said the old man. "Go on, boy. Take the candle with you."

He put his hand on my shoulder and gave me a little push. I marvelled at his coolness, until I remembered that he would not be able to come with me. Still I knew that this thought was unjust, and that if he had been only a little smaller he would have been in the inner cave long before now, instead of sitting there, as I was, shivering at the idea of risking my skin.

"Here goes!" I said loudly, to frighten the monster.

We edged the boat over to the stone organ-pipes. It grounded gently on the rocky floor of the cave. Even since we had come in, the tide had dropped a little more, as we could see by the glistening walls.

I got an arm around one of the ridges, to steady myself. Then I poked my head through the biggest space, and my other arm, holding the candle, through the next. I saw a fine, high vaulted cave with a floor of rock lightly sprinkled with silver sand and strange flat shells.

"It's as dry as a threshing-floor," I said with a sudden burst of courage. "I'm going in."

And without further delay I climbed through the space and dropped on the floor.

"Watch your step!"

My grandfather's voice came to me in a half-whisper. When I answered him I found that my own voice was the same, through some curious trick of the formation of the roof. As I walked a few steps forward I found that I could no longer hear the friendly beating of the sea, nor the seagulls' sharp cries. But the hum of the breeze through the stone pipes sounded louder than it had done from outside.

I lifted my candle and looked all around me. I was astonished at the smoothness of the floor, with its neat carpet of sand. The walls showed no drip nor trickle of water. I suppose that the sea's level must have dropped since the days when it had carved out this great hole in the cliff's side.

Towards the back, the cave took a turn and narrowed, and its roof sloped a little downwards. I walked on, somewhat disappointed now, that there was no more mystery. Then all at once I stopped. I think I gave a shout, but if I did, it died on that dim air and was swallowed up in the shadowy spaces around me. For several minutes I stood quite still, until the hot grease of the candle spilled over on to my hand and brought me to my senses again. Then I took one more step and gazed down at my find.

It was the long narrow hull of a wooden boat. It had not rotted, but had shrivelled up and fallen apart. Only its prow still stood, carved with a dragon's head, propped between two big stones. And leaning back against it as if he were tired, were the huge bones of a man. He wore a bronze helmet, decorated with short, straight horns. His bony fingers lay listlessly on the hilt of a long sword. Thus he had sat I supposed, for a thousand years, exactly as his friends had left him.

After my first surprise I could see that this was the tomb of a Viking. There was no

mistaking that horned helmet. When I was a
small boy at school, our teacher had described
so vividly the raids of the Norsemen on the
Irish coast that for many months my dreams
were alive with narrow, black-beaked galleys
full of horned warriors, darting up our rivers,
pillaging our monasteries and towns and
bearing away our people to slavery. But I had
never thought that I would see a Viking face
to face.

I went a little closer, and then I saw the
gaming board. It may have been placed on his
knees once, so that he could amuse himself
during his long waiting time. It had fallen
down long since, and now it lay on the ground
between the shrivelled limbs of the boat.

I had never seen a board like it before. It
was square, and rather like a board for playing
draughts, which is a favourite game with us.
It was made of a thick block of wood, carved
all around the edges with an intricate pattern
of snakes nibbling at each other's tails.

I stooped down and lifted it very carefully,
with some idea, I suppose, that it might fall
into dust in my hands. I saw at once, however,
that it was tough and strong. Only a tiny
crack at one side showed how the moisture
had dried out of it, so that it had warped a

very little. I held the candle close and examined it.

At either side a carved head projected, like handles. One was the head of a man, flat-nosed, with a longish, surprised face and a tiny pointed beard. The other was the head of a wolf, with pointed ears and snarling lips and little, terrible round eyes. But the thing that charmed me most was that all over the board, arranged in even rows, were tiny carved bone figures. They did not stand on squares as draughts and chessmen do, but each piece was finished with a short peg which fitted into a corresponding hole in the board. I discovered that this was so when I lifted a piece to find out why they had not all fallen over. All of the pieces were little wolves' heads, except one which was the head of a man. This was placed in the exact middle of the board, and the wolves filled the remainder, in rows of seven by seven. There was an extra hole in each corner, but each of these was marked off with a segment of a circle so that I guessed there were no pieces missing.

With a gentle finger, I stroked the little wolf's head that I was holding. In all my life I had never loved anything so much. It was a satin-smooth, close-textured bone, clean and polished so that it reflected little points of light from the candle. For a while I forgot that I was in an uncharted cave half under the sea. The children in my part of the world do not have many toys—most of our games were played with stones and sticks that can be picked up anywhere on a day's walk. This only meant that I could see the possibilities of the Viking's game all the more clearly. I knew that I would not need to be shown how to play it. One could invent a dozen ways. The man, of course, was trying to escape from the wolves into one of the four corners. So the wolves must make the first move, or else the man must sometimes be allowed to jump over them.

Suddenly as I was settling down to play the game, I remembered my grandfather. He could have been calling to me for minutes past, and that I did not hear him. It was all so silent in the cave. He would be frightened for my safety. He might even have started back to Barrinish to rouse the neighbours to dig me out. Then our discovery would be a secret no longer. Someone else might even get my board. Carrying it carefully, I hurried back to the cave mouth.

The old man was still there. He was calling me, sure enough, peering anxiously through the stone pipes. He looked relieved when he saw my candle-flame. Without waiting to climb through into the currach, I tumbled out the story of my finds.

"And whoever arranged the cave did a tasty job," I said. "Beautiful clean sand sprinkled everywhere like the sawdust on the floor of Corny Lynch's shop, and shells of some strange fish, that I never saw the like of before. I wish you could come in and see the boat and the old soldier sitting back in it."

"God rest his bones!" said my grandfather. "What have you there in your hand?"

I showed him the board. Like me, he was delighted beyond measure at the neat, smooth little figures.

"We'll have many a game with those on the long winter nights," I said eagerly. "We'll make our own rules, but once they're made, we must keep to them."

He was silent for a moment. Uneasily I asked:

"Won't we be able to have it for ourselves? Who has a better right to it than us? What is it, anyway, but a game? A game couldn't be so very important."

Even while I made one excuse after another, I was beginning to realise a little of the excitement that would be caused by the discovery of the Viking and his board. We were not so ignorant as to imagine that people all over the world would not hear about him in time, and that historians and archaeologists would not be ready to tear out each other's hair because of him. We knew of these things because Mr Allen often spoke of them.

He was the last of his family, who had once owned all the islands and the good land in our district. He still owned the big house over near Cashel, but it was gone to rack and ruin, and he preferred to live alone in a little cottage at the far end of Barrinish Island from us. Mr Allen and my grandfather were good friends. Whenever he visited our house, his talk opened up great new roads for me so that I was never the same again after he had gone away. Sometimes I went with my grandfather to visit him, and this was even better, for his house was full of curiosities and books of a kind that I have never since seen anywhere else. He had a way that pleased me very much, of turning to me and explaining some point in the discussion that might have been too difficult for me. I had a great respect for his learning, and it was natural that I should suggest now that we should ask him for help and advice.

"Yes," said my grandfather. "Mr Allen will know what is to be done. He's a fine man of knowledge. Now just put the board back where you found it and we'll be going home."

We argued for a long time about this. Of course I wanted to bring the board home with me, and show it to my great friend, Tom Joyce, and play a few games in the evenings, under the admiring eyes of the men. Already I was glorying in the prospect of being a great hero, the owner of this wonderful treasure and the one person who would decide who was to play with it next. Patiently my grandfather pointed out that if we took it home and showed it to the people, we would have to say where we had found it. Even if we managed to keep the existence of the inner cave a secret, the board itself was such a curiosity that it would almost certainly bring crowds of strangers nosing about, asking questions and even going foraging for themselves.

"There's no end to what they might find," said the old man. "It wouldn't be hard for them to find the Clooney Cave, or the new still over at Achadown. If they do, the people of this parish won't be a bit thankful to us, you may go bail."

That settled the question for me. The Clooney Cave was at the outermost part of the island. It served us all as a warehouse in which to hide the wrack that we rescued from the sea, which by a stupid old law we were supposed to hand over to the Guards. We had no qualms of conscience about keeping the wrack. If we did not bring in the baulks of timber and bales of cloth and barrels of oil and meal that were sent to us by the sea, they would all be broken up and destroyed by the waves among the rocks, and then no one would have the benefit of them. What man would be foolish enough to risk his neck and his good boat to bring in wrack for the Guards, that never get their feet wet if they can help it? So we laid all the stuff away in Clooney Cave until we could use it a little at a time. As for the new still, I had heard the men say that the best poiteen in Connemara was coming lately from Achadown. Of course they could not afford to buy whiskey with the prices that the robbers of shopkeepers were charging, and a man needs a drop of spirits after a long night on the sea or a long day drawing weed, or on the bog.

"'Tis true for you," I said reluctantly. "It's easy enough to turn one or two people away from those places, but we could never manage a crowd." I felt my heart squeeze dry as a new thought occurred to me. "What will we do if the tide comes up and fills the cave, and washes away the boat and the board and the old Viking? How do we know that won't happen?"

"When it didn't happen in the storm it won't happen on the tide," said my grandfather. "When you were inside the cave, I wasn't idle. You left the matches behind you, and I used them to find out something that was puzzling me. Tell me now, did you wonder how they got the boat and the man into that cave the day long ago?"

My astonished face told him plainly that I had not thought of this at all. He chuckled at my expression.

"Hold that candle high," he said, "and I'll show you. This whole gateway, as you might say, closing up the cave, is not natural at all. There's marks of a chisel here at the sides where the stone was chipped off so that the stone grid would fit. And the grid is made in several pieces. Look at the joins. I'd swear there's a tongue and groove holding them together. The wonder is that they held so long. Then the pieces that had fallen out, look at them lying on the floor inside. See how their edges are all thinned off, to fit into the long spaces."

I peered at them and saw that this was so.

"First they brought the boat and the old Viking and fixed him up inside," my grandfather went on. "Then they put up the grid, and last of all they filled in the spaces with stone. And I wish I knew why they went to all that bother, when they could have buried him decent, like a Christian, above in Cluan na Marbh."

"They weren't Christians," I said. "They believed in Valhalla, and gods of thunder and storm. Maybe that's why they made the pipes, so that the wind could sing through them. It was queer that they went to the trouble of blocking up the spaces then. Maybe Mr Allen will be able to tell us that too."

"Back with the board, then, and we'll be going home."

I turned without a word and went back into the depths of the cave. Very softly, I replaced the precious board in the exact position in which I had found it. I stood for a moment looking down at it, and wondering if I would slip a few of the little wolves' heads into my pocket. But though I would cheerfully have taken the whole board it seemed wrong to break up the perfection of the game.

I did not run on the way out. It was a friendly place, though it was so strange. I climbed out through the stone grid and into the currach. A moment later we were out in the sweet blue air again, and heading for home.

3

We Visit Mr Allen

ack at the house, we fed the chickens and ducks and turkeys, and milked the Kerry cow. She hated to be kept waiting, and she kept tossing her head and turning to glare at me resentfully while I milked her. When I had almost finished, she flicked her long dusty tail expertly into the milk and then across my face, and strolled off sniggering.

After dinner we harnessed the horse, and set off for Mr Allen's house. To get there we had to go down the hill, through the village and out on to the long curving bleak road that leads to the bridge, connecting Barrinish with Brosna. As we clattered along through the clear afternoon air, the people working in the fields called out to us on a high carrying note:

"Hoy, Mick Cooney! Hoy, Patcheen! Going off gallivanting while the rest of us work! Some people have a fine life. Ye'll be around to us for a loan of a bucket of spuds in the tail-end of the winter!"

This they said for the fun of rousing the old man; they all knew that he would not borrow as much as a puffin's egg, he was so fiercely independent. He bridled now, to their great delight, and shouted back to them:

"We won't need to borrow. We have enough spuds set to feed the island. We were out working when the rest of ye were hanging over the fire, thinking it was still winter!"

By the time he had finished this speech, we had passed out of range of their shouts of laughter. The old man sat back, gripping his knees and breathing fast with vexation. The cart bounced along, for the horse was lively this fine day. At the end of the bare acres of stone and rock and sedge that form the nether tip of the island, Mr Allen's cottage stood looking down towards the bridge.

It was a stone cottage, built on the side of the road, but though it was only one story high it was a little bigger and better finished than most of our neighbours'. It had belonged to the Allens' land-agent once. It was sheltered all around with an old grove of Scotch firs. These were the only big trees on the island and they set Mr Allen's cottage apart from ours more surely than any other detail could have done. It never occurred to us that we could easily have grown trees of our own.

By the side of the cottage there was a lean-to cart-shed with a floor of turf-mould. Its roof was an old wooden boat turned upside down, with its keel pointing to the sky. When you were in the shed, you looked up at the thwarts of the boat, now being used for hanging harness and ropes. My grandfather had tried many times to get Mr Allen to build a proper shed, that strangers would not stop and laugh when they saw it. But Mr Allen said he liked it as it was and he would not change it.

We backed the cart into the shed so that the horse would be sheltered from the nibbling little wind. As I was hitching the reins to a ring in the gable-end of the house I saw Mr Allen's housekeeper peeking through the glass of the porch at us. She nipped out of sight again at once, probably thinking that neither of us had seen her.

I had been well schooled by my grandfather in his honest ways, and for this reason I

resented being peeked at. Besides, I knew
that she was not doing it so that she could
hurry into the kitchen and put on the kettle
to make tea for us. She was the sort of
woman who counts the grains of tea going
into the pot, even if it is not her own tea. Her
name was Sarah Conneeley, and she was a
married woman from a village called Le Clé
on the mainland. Le Clé simply means "on
the left-hand side." There were seven houses
in that village, and the man of every house
happened to be called Seán. Sarah's Seán was
a sailor, so that he was away from home for
many months of every year. Her brother was
the Captain of the *Saint Ronan*, the Breton
lobster-boat that came around every few weeks
to collect lobsters from all the islands. She
had no children, so she was free to come and
look after Mr Allen. He had taught her how to
cook the kind of food that he liked, and she
kept the wooden floors of the cottage polished
like old gold. But this made her feel a little
bit grand, I think, so that she had come to
imagine herself a cut above the rest of us.
Still she wore the red flannel petticoat that
all the women wear in these parts. The wives
of the other six Seáns saw to that. In appearance she was like a hungry thrush. She ate a

great deal, smiling gently all the time in her satisfaction.

Though she had seen us, she kept us waiting on the doorstep for several minutes after we had knocked. The door stood wide, of course, so that we could see directly into the sitting-room into which the porch opened. There was a good fire and an open book on the table beside it, so we knew that Mr Allen was not far away. Presently Sarah came strolling leisurely through from the kitchen.

"Good evening to you, Sarah," said my grandfather eagerly, taking her hand and shaking it vigorously. "Fresh and well you're looking, a-girl. Were you home lately? How are the seven Seáns?"

All seven were great friends of his. Visiting Le Clé took a whole day, because a certain amount of time had to be spent in each house.

"I wasn't home for a few weeks," said Sarah coolly. "Are you wanting to come in?"

"Sure of course! You don't think we came this far just to stand looking in the doorway," said the old man heartily, marching into the room.

She looked with disfavour at our boots, but she did not dare to tell us to wipe them.

"I'll tell Mr Allen," she said. "He's out in

the field."

When she had gone, the old man said philosophically:

"She hasn't a word to throw to a dog, but she's good-hearted enough, is Sarah."

I doubted this last, but I said nothing, for I never liked to make my grandfather uneasy with his neighbours.

Within a few minutes Mr Allen came in. He was not a small man, but he was stooped at the knees and the shoulders in a way that made him seem so. His hair was grey, curling upwards and outwards in little tufts. His eyebrows and his moustache curled too, so that at first sight he had an appearance of perpetual good humour. But I always thought his eyes were melancholy. He was usually dressed in a sand-coloured tweed suit, almost the colour of his tired face. My grandfather said he was no more than sixty, but to me he looked as old as Noah. He came towards us with both hands outstretched.

"Ah, my friends! You are welcome. Do sit down."

We knew him well enough not to be put out at his stiff way of speech. We sat down in two súgán chairs which though they looked exactly the same as those we had at home, somehow

always seemed more comfortable. My grandfather began at once:

"We've got great news for you, Mr Allen,
great news."

He rubbed his hands together with a little
crowing chuckle.

"Ha! Now you'll have to agree that we have
the name of our bay right. Norseman's Bay it
is. Now I can prove it up to the hilt!"

"Horseman's Bay," Mr Allen corrected him,
shaking his head and smiling. "Only yesterday I met a man who said that the old Irish
name is Cuan an Mharcaigh and that is
Horseman's Bay."

"That man is a liar," said my grandfather
delightedly, "or else he was only saying it to
please you."

A flicker of anger at this notion passed
over Mr Allen's face, but my grandfather did
not notice it. He was saying:

"Norseman's Bay, and the old Irish name
for it is Cuan na nGall, and that's the name
everyone here has on it. But wait till we tell
you what we found and you'll have to believe
it yourself."

"A Viking sword in a bog, I suppose, brought
here from County Meath in the seventeenth
century, by someone on the run from

Cromwell," said Mr Allen, speaking in little quick gasps.

"We found a sword, all right," said my grandfather, "and a Viking with it!"

He leaned back to observe the effect of this. Mr Allen said softly:

"You found a Viking? Dead or alive?"

"Dead, man! As dead as Finn MacCool! Go on, Pat. Tell him all about it."

I described how I had been up on the cliff-top when the cave began to sing, and how we had gone around in the currach when the storm died down and found the cause of it. Then I told him how I had climbed into the inner cave and had come upon the Viking sitting in his boat. Mr Allen had been looking at me in the condescending way that one might look at a man who was a bit soft in the head, but now he seemed suddenly to take me more seriously.

"So you are the only person who has seen this Viking?" he said, looking at me directly.

"Yes," I said. "The way into the cave is small."

He turned a little away from me and addressed my grandfather.

"That's probably a smuggler who hid there, with his boat, from the Revenue officers. He

must have been taken ill and died in the cave.
Perhaps he was not able to get out. By your
description of the place, it was not easy to get
in and out. The Vikings never came to this
part of Ireland. I've made a great study of
that time. I've written several books about it,
as you know. That was no Viking."

"It was a Viking, all right," I said sharply,
for I did not like the little smile that Mr Allen
was turning on me now. "His bones were old,
old. He had a big helmet on, with horns. His
boat was carved with a dragon's head. His
sword was right by his hand. He was no
smuggler."

"And there is the game he had with him,"
said my grandfather, coming to my support,
though he had sent me a warning look to
mend my manners.

"A game?"

"I saw that myself," said the old man
eagerly. "Pat brought it out of the back of the
cave and showed it to me. It's a marvel. It's
one of the seven wonders. I never saw the
beat of it, all the little wolves' heads and they
carved out in bone, shiny and polished by the
hands of men that are under the sod this
thousand years. That's a Norseman's game,
as you told me yourself. 'Twas from all you

told me that I recognised it."

Now that he had proved his point my grandfather was trying in his kindly way to give some of the credit for the find to Mr Allen. I was uneasy too, for I felt that I should have been more civil. Mr Allen seemed to have accepted our story. Now we were glad to see his old friendly smile again as he asked:

"Have you brought the board with you?"

"No, no. I told Pat to put it back in the cave where he found it. We want you to come and see it, because you'll be able to tell the whole world about it. We'll have to break down a piece of the stonework to get in, but that can't be helped. We'll bring a chisel and do a right neat job on it. When will you be able to come?"

"Not before tomorrow," said Mr Allen. "The wind is too strong for me today. My stomach would not stand the sea, I'm afraid."

"Be hanged to your stomach," said the old man impatiently. "You couldn't wait till tomorrow. You'd never close an eye in sleep tonight for thinking of it all."

It was clear enough that my grandfather was the one who would not close an eye in sleep, until he would have had the satisfaction of showing the Viking and his possessions to Mr Allen. But we could not persuade him to come.

"No, no, no," he said. "If that Viking has waited a thousand years, he can surely wait one night more."

With that we had to be satisfied. As we drove home my grandfather shook his head in astonishment at Mr Allen's philosophy.

"I don't understand him at all," he complained to me. "What fun is there in life if we never hurry? Hurrying is excitement, and excitement is something happening, and something happening is life itself. I don't understand it."

Throughout the evening he would pause, and snort, and then shake his head again and say, in a sardonic imitation of Mr Allen's voice:

"The Viking will wait! He'll wait one night more! There's a man for you! I believe he wouldn't bother to come out on his own doorstep to see the Angel Gabriel blow the last trump. 'Time enough,' he'd say. 'Time enough.'"

But the Viking did not wait.

In the morning, I could no longer contain my impatience. I got out our smaller currach before my grandfather was awake. I took a line and a jar of bait for appearances' sake, and sat in the currach, half beached on the shingly strand, munching thick slices of soda-bread for my breakfast and thinking about why I was going so early and alone. Mr Allen had made me uneasy. All night long, awake and asleep, I had brooded about it, so that I had almost begun to wonder whether my Viking were not after all a poor thief who had crept in there somehow and had been unable to come out. Now I wished I had brought away the game, in spite of my grandfather's arguments. It would have been a comfort to have been able to handle the little pieces. To me they proved even more clearly than did the horned helmet that the man belonged to another age. Above all I resented Mr Allen's indifference. I supposed it was because he was old, and a sort of coldness came over me at the thought of drying up like that one day. Then I remembered my grandfather, with his bubbling enthusiasm, and I felt a little better. Too much education perhaps, I thought, had drained the joy of life out of Mr Allen.

Presently I stepped ashore and pushed the currach gently afloat. Here in the shelter the sea was smooth and calm. The storm had left great heaps of weed lying about on the beach, and right beside the currach a little carpet of tiny coloured shells, like jewels, pink and yellow and brown and a pale, delicate purple. Those shells were to us what marbles are to most children. We had learned to count with them at school, and had made beautiful patterned picture-frames for the photographs from America, by sticking them on to cardboard. There was hardly a boy on the island who did not own a collection of several hundreds of them.

As I rowed softly out between the rocks, I kept a sharp eye out for some green glass floats to replace those that had been broken on the night of the storm. Sure enough, I found two, cradled in bladder wrack on the rocks, and took them on board. There was always a special thrill in finding these, smooth and round and glittering and always in some strange way unexpected. After I had found them I had no further excuse for delay. I rowed on slowly under the shadow of the cliffs, and presently I slipped into the Singing Cave.

I moored the boat to one of the rocky bars. Immediately I saw that the opening through which I had entered the inner cave had widened since yesterday. It had been a calm night for April, with only a little swell at sea. Still I thought it possible that once the grid had begun to fall down it would continue to do so, little by little, until the inner cave would become part of the outer one. I wondered too if the seals could have broken the stone, so as to use the cave to sleep in. I knew very little about the habits of seals. There were hundreds of them around our coast. They broke our nets and stole the fish and then slipped away under water when we went out after them with guns. But though we spoke of them as crafty, wicked creatures, I could not imagine their being able to tear down a wall of stone with their soft, helpless-looking flippers.

There was no time to be wasted now in wondering what had happened. Today I was not afraid to climb through into the inner cave. Just inside, I paused to light the candle-end that I had brought with me. The first thing I saw was that many of the flat shells that covered the sandy floor were ground into powder. I had broken some yesterday, but only a few. Now it was clear that since then several heavy people had trampled about. I saw the blurred print of a sea-boot in the

silver sand. One wall had a light streak of
fresh soot from a lantern.

I looked around me in a daze, hardly be-
lieving yet that my worst fears had come
true. Slowly I turned and walked through to
the back of the cave. It was quite empty. For
several minutes I stared stupidly at the place
where the Viking and his boat had been, as if
by looking long and hard enough I could bring
them back again. Every scrap of timber was
gone. A line scarred in the sand showed where
the sword had lain. Not a bone of the Viking
remained, though I scoured the sand again
and again in the hope of finding some trace of
him. I looked for the little wolves' heads too,
though I remembered that their pegs had
fitted too neatly into the holes in the board
for them to drop easily out. Besides I knew
that whoever had taken them away would be
specially watchful of this part of the find
because of its strangeness. I did not yet want
to think of who this person might be.

All at once a kind of sickness came over me
at the uselessness of grubbing here in the
sand. My head ached from stooping. I had
singed my hair with the candle, holding it too
close to peer at the ground. The rank, un-
pleasant smell of it seemed to fill the cave to

suffocation. Slowly I came out as far as the stone grid. With my new knowledge, it was easy to see now that it had been broken with sledges and chisels.

Slowly I climbed into the currach and eased myself out of the cave. I wished that the journey home were seven times as long as it was. All the way back to the beach I practised aloud different ways of breaking the news to my grandfather. I even thought of concealing the fact that I had been to the cave this morning. I could go out with him in the currach later on, and let him lead the way in through the broken grid, and then when he would come upon the empty floor where the Viking had been, I could feign astonishment, anger, disgust. Yes, that was the very best way, I felt sure.

But when I had beached the boat, some demon suddenly took possession of my legs so that I bounded up over the rocks as if I were on springs. I never stopped till I stood in the open doorway of the kitchen. A gold bar of sunlight fell across the table where my grandfather had laid breakfast for both of us. He was putting the teapot to draw on a hot coal by the fire. He looked up, startled at my sudden appearance.

"Pat. What's happened?"

"Our old Viking, the gaming board, the boat with the dragon's head, the sword and all—they're gone!"

4

We Do Some Spying

e sat over that table
until noon. Many times,
I described to him the
condition in which I had found the cave. I
wanted him to come out there at once and
lament over it with me, but he would not.

"Later on I'll go," he said. "First we must
think. Did anyone see us going out to the cave
yesterday?"

"There wasn't a soul abroad but ourselves,"
said I.

He thought that someone must have heard
the cave singing and have gone out as we had
done to find the cause of it.

"It could be that we were no sooner gone
from it than they came and broke into the
cave and took all the things away to safety.
Maybe the Viking is sitting in the Clooney

Cave this minute."

"Maybe so," I said doubtfully. "But surely we'd have heard about it by now."

"We didn't do much talking ourselves," my grandfather pointed out. "And we had no visitors last night. The whole island could be humming with that story now and us none the wiser."

"We told no one but Mr Allen," I said.

The old man sighed.

"And now we're going to look mighty foolish telling him that there's no need at all for him to come to the cave. We should have boxed up the whole lot and landed it in the door to him yesterday."

I made no reply to this. My grandfather went on:

" 'Twould remind you of a true saying that was in our red poetry-book at school long ago: 'Of all sad words of tongue or pen, the saddest are: "It might have be'n." ' "

I always knew he was really upset when he began to quote from the red poetry-book.

"If the Viking is in Clooney, we won't be long finding him," I said. "Let's go over there now. We can get out the timber for the new gate while we're at it."

We had a store of planks there, on which

we drew from time to time for various purposes. We took the horse and cart with us, and set out for Clooney. I knew quite well that we would find nothing there, but still I was glad to be searching actively for my Viking at last. There was an aching loneliness in my bones for him, which I could not quite understand, but which made me determined to find him wherever he might be.

All the way out to Clooney my grandfather sorrowed over the disappointment that Mr Allen would feel when he would hear that the cave had been raided and that he had missed the find of the century. I was only a boy, and not a very patient one. Only a few weeks before, I had boxed another boy's ears because he had differed with me about the proper way to bait a hook. To this day I do not know how I held my tongue. Hold it I did, while we went diligently through every item in the cave searching, searching for anything that might look like a Viking. He was not there, of course.

On the way home with our planks we took the inland road so as to call on Rooster Hernon. He lived with his sister Kate, a tall, thin, loose-jointed, plunging woman, very like Rooster in appearance but that her hair was black. Everyone called her the Snipe, but not to her face. She was a kindly soul. She put on a clean apron and made tea for us at once, and sat down at the table to show that she did not mind how long we stayed. Presently Rooster came in. He was at ease now, because he was in his own house.

"Ha! Visitors!" he said, while he was still on the doorstep. " 'Tis a terrible thing to live in an out-of-the-way place like this. Would you believe that sometimes half a day does pass without anyone walking in on the floor to us? Amn't I right, Kate?"

" 'Tis true for you," said Kate. " 'Tis indeed."

"Anything could be happening on the island," Rooster complained, "and we'd be the last to hear it. There's the *Saint Ronan* below at the quay for the last two hours and I only heard it this minute from Carroll's Julia going home from school. Isn't it a fright to the world when the children can tell their elders a piece of news like that?"

We agreed that it was, though we knew that Rooster's fear of being left out of things made him the best-informed man in the island.

"I didn't know that the *Saint Ronan* was there," said my grandfather, "and I living within a stone's throw of the quay."

"You didn't, of course," said Rooster, "but how could you when you were over at Clooney getting out planks to make a gate?"

We had mentioned this purpose to one man only, Batt Faherty, who had been at the cave fetching out a bale of sheet rubber to roof his cow-house.

"Did you hear how long the *Saint Ronan* is staying?" my grandfather asked.

"No," said Rooster regretfully. "Carroll's Julia has no nose for news. You'd think that would be the first thing she'd ask. But all that was troubling her was to go home and tell her father to bring down his lobsters quick and sell them."

"The lobsters were the most important," said the Snipe admiringly. "Julia is a well-trained child."

"She is, I suppose," said Rooster without enthusiasm. "But knowledge is power, and it wouldn't have killed her to have waited for the rest of the news. Now I'll have to go down to the quay myself and have a chat with Big Dan Moloney and find out a few necessary things."

His nose twitched at the prospect. By this time it was plain enough that he had heard nothing about the Viking nor the Singing Cave. If he had he would have told us about it at once. With Rooster, news was not news until it had been passed on.

He made no attempt to hurry us, but he watched anxiously while we drank our tea. As I drained my cup for the third time he said to my grandfather:

"I'll take a drive from you down to the quay, Mick. I might have a few lobsters for Big Dan myself."

The Snipe came to the door and waved to us while we drove away. I had the reins. While the two men told each other exactly how their crops were faring, I was able to brood undisturbed on the possibility that we would never be able to prove who had rifled the Singing Cave. I had a deep respect for my grandfather, but I could see that this time his innocence was his undoing. It offended me to see him being cheated so easily. Craft and determination were necessary now, and I feared that neither he nor I had a proper share of them.

Long before we reached the quay I had decided to tell the whole story to Tom Joyce. He was my best friend, but though he was the same age as myself he knew a great deal more about the big world than I did. This was because he often spent a few days in Galway with his Aunt Minnie. She kept the restaurant to which all the islanders used to go for a meal on fair days. What Tom did not learn from listening to the customers' talk he learned from his Aunt Minnie. She was a huge, comfortable woman, the breadth of the door as we say, and she had a huge, comfortable mind. She had lived in Boston for many years. She knew every virtue and every failing of which man is capable, and she was always able to illustrate them with tales of people she knew on one side of the Atlantic or the other. Thus Tom had acquired a great store of second-hand wisdom. Now was his chance of putting it to practical use.

I had little doubt that I would find him at the quay. Sure enough, his black head was the first thing I saw as we clattered down over the big flagstones in the cart. He had a catch of lobsters and was waiting his turn to hand them over to Big Dan Moloney. A sort of counter had been erected, of a plank laid on two barrels, and Big Dan stood by like a judge at a pony show while the lobsters were paraded before him. No one liked Big Dan, but he gave fair prices for lobsters. This was easy for him, since the money was not his own. He was an Achill Island man. His sister, as I have said, was Mr Allen's housekeeper.

Rooster was calling out before the horse stopped:

"Hoy, Big Dan! The old tub is still floating!"

"She is, Rooster, she is," said Big Dan. "Sorro' fear of her!"

But he kept his eye on the lobsters that were being counted into a crate by the three Breton sailors who formed the crew of his ship.

I tied the reins to a ring in the quay wall and went over to talk to Tom.

"Get rid of those lobsters quick," I said to him. "I have something to tell you."

"You can't get rid of lobsters quick," said Tom firmly. "Go down on to the boat and I'll be after you in a few minutes."

I swallowed my impatience and went down to the *Saint Ronan*. No one took any notice of me. Every boy on the island boarded the *Saint Ronan* when she came in, because she was the strangest boat one could imagine. Amidships there was no bottom to her, but only a steel cage through which the sea flowed. In there the lobsters were put, and brought back alive to France. Most of them ended their days in Paris, where, Big Dan said, the people are very particular about their food. Gazing down through the water in the tank, the floor of the sea was a silky, luminous green. I waited for Tom below in the quiet, listening to the soft splash of the sea against the little ship's side. By the time that I heard his cautious feet on the companionway the stillness had calmed me. This was a good thing; Tom had no patience with excitable people. His first words were:

"Talk up, man! There's no one on the boat but ourselves. They're all out on the quay with the lobsters."

I could not resist teasing his curiosity by asking:

"Did you get a good price for yours?"

"Enough to make it worth while going for more," said Tom. "What have you been up to? You look like someone that has met the pooka."

"He wasn't a pooka," I said sadly, remembering my big, bony friend.

I told him the whole story. At the end I said:

"And there's only one person in these parts who could have been so quick and clever and silent in opening up the cave and taking him away."

"Mr Allen," said Tom softly.

"You can see that as plain as a pikestaff, and my grandfather can't," I said angrily. "He's going over this evening to apologise to Mr Allen because we have nothing to show him after all."

We could think of no reason why Mr Allen had not allowed my grandfather the pleasure of showing him the cave.

"A mean, cold look came over his face when we were telling him about it," I remembered. "At first he would hardly believe that the story was true. Then, even after he had accepted it, he was in no hurry to come and see for himself. He said it was because of his stomach. But he never lets his stomach stand in the way of a thing he wants to do."

"One thing is certain," said Tom after a moment. "He didn't do it alone. He's an old man. He would have had to have help. One man can keep silent forever. Two men can't."

I knew by the sound of this statement that it must have come from Aunt Minnie.

"There's sense in that," I said, "but I'd like if they would talk soon."

It was maddening to be able to do nothing but wait. As long as the lobster-buying went on, the little crowd stayed on the quay. We moved through them, listening intently for an incautious word dropped by mistake, or a quick gesture betraying suppressed excitement, or even a knowing confidential pair of looks exchanged. But all of our neighbours were exactly the same as usual, full of drawling, half-humorous talk which we thought they could not have assumed if they had been out all night on extraordinary business. Not one man mentioned the name of the Singing Cave.

When the crowd broke up we separated. There was hardly a house on Barrinish which did not have a visit from either one or the other of us that afternoon. We divided the island between us. I took the western part, for I did not want to meet Mr Allen nor his Sarah; Tom had more courage for them, because he did not know them so well. In each house we sat for a polite quarter of an hour on the hob and ate a polite slice of soda-bread and butter, and listened to the family's talk. I was a bit worried about the bread and butter, but Tom said that was nonsense.

"If we refuse their hospitality, we might as well walk in the door announcing that we're spies," he said. "This is serious business. We can't afford to be squeamish. Besides, if the people knew what we are about, they would want to help us. It's a pity that we can't tell them."

"No, we'd better not tell them yet."

When we met in the evening down by the quay, we had learned nothing at all.

"Nothing useful, that is," said Tom. "I've learned that Sally George's daughter has twin babies in Portland, and Corny Lynch is going to build a new wool store on to the shop, and Lord Folan and Mattie Connor are thinking of building a new hooker between them."

"And Carroll's Julia cut her toe on a glass bottle on the road home with the story about the lobsters," said I, "and two strange men that might have been excise men have been for a sail around Golam, and Master Murphy says he's going to have a melodeon band in the school next year. I wonder could we go back to school for that."

"The trouble would be to get out again when the band practice would be over," Tom pointed out. "My Aunt Minnie always says it's not always as easy to get out of a thing as it is to get in."

We sat on the quay wall in the late evening sun. Neither of us needed to go home for a meal, because we were packed as tight as pups with soda-bread.

"My grandfather is gone over to Mr Allen's now," I said presently. "There won't be any fun in our house tonight. As soon as the men find that he's not in, they'll all walk down to the tailor's."

"Then we'll go down to the tailor's now and we'll be there before them."

We slipped down off the wall and started for the tailor's house. This was the very tailor who had nearly got me as an apprentice. He lived in the village. His house was always brilliantly whitewashed and well thatched. He employed other people to do this work for him because he could not do it himself on account of his lame leg. His garden was full of wallflowers and fat pink cabbage-roses, which he tended with his own hands. It was the only work he did besides making clothes for every man and boy in the four islands. He was not overworked—we like to get ten years out of a suit in the islands. Still he had to spend his evenings sitting cross-legged on his table, stitching intently and without ceasing, no matter how many visitors he might have. I suppose it was not a cheerful life. He loved to have visitors, and was blackly jealous of my grandfather at this time for attracting the men to our house in the evenings. I did not know this, for the tailor had never shown me the smallest hint of it.

He was sitting in his usual place on the table when we went in. He had a soft, gentle voice; I think now, looking back after many years, that he was not a very healthy man. He said:

"Come in, boys, come in. Another storm coming, I'd say. Put a sod on the fire there, Tom, and we'll be comfortable."

Only one other man was there before us. I thought that the reason for our hearty welcome might have been that the tailor was finding his visitor difficult. It was old Johnny Gill.

Johnny was an oddity. Most people said he was "a man of God," which is their delicate way of saying that he was not right in the head. But I always thought that there was more to Johnny than he pretended. I went to some trouble to treat him very carefully, as if he were as sound as any of my neighbours. This made him more fond of me than I liked. He jumped off the hob now and insisted that I sit in there while he brought over a creepy stool for himself. He sat down, close enough to be able to nudge me with his knee whenever he felt like it.

Tom and the tailor started to talk about the sports that we were going to have in Barrinish in a week's time.

"Sports!" said Johnny contemptuously to me while I strained my ears towards the other pair. "Sports and circuses and currach-races! Children's games! Those things are not for grown men. 'Twould be fitter for them to be thinking of death, for there's death and disaster coming to Barrinish."

In spite of his lugubrious words he gave a little happy chuckle at the prospect. He nudged me with his knee and his elbow and leaned even closer. "Did I ever tell you about the five things in the life of man? Did I? Did I?"

"No, Johnny. You didn't," I said.

"Five things," said Johnny, lifting a handful of fingers to count them. "Birth, growth, maturity, death and decay." He leaned a little backwards to look at me triumphantly. "Aren't they fine, gentlemanly words? Birth, growth, maturity," he rolled it on his tongue, as if he were tasting it, "death and decay."

"True for you, Johnny," said I amicably.

"You're a clever boy," said Johnny. "And I'll tell you how I know there's death coming to Barrinish." Again he was nudging and leaning close. He lowered his voice to a whisper. "The long cart passed by my house, on the old road over the mountains. Whenever a cart passes on the old road, it's a sign of death. But I'm not afraid of death, because I know about the five things. I followed the cart. I did." This time I nudged him first, so that he looked at me with plain delight. " 'Twas black as the pit, but I followed it until they chased me away. I cursed them for that, black curses and red curses and yellow curses—"

I was listening to him now with all my ears, you may be sure.

"What was on the long cart, Johnny?" I asked, almost choking in my efforts to appear unconcerned.

" 'Twas too dark for me to see."

He cocked his head on one side and burst into a wild cackle of laughter. I picked up a sod and laid it on the fire as if I had lost interest in him. He clawed at my sleeve so that I felt his nails through the wool of my jersey.

" 'Twas too dark to see right," he said softly. "But I know the devil was on that cart. I saw horns!"

5

We Talk with Louan

"**G**od bless my soul, Johnny!" I exclaimed. "Horns!"

"Ay," said Johnny. "Horns are queer-looking things, but they are useful. They must be grand for fighting with."

He lowered his head and tossed it as if he were threatening me with imaginary horns. I tried to bring him back to the story of the long cart, but he just looked at me slyly and said:

"Did I ever tell you how they found out the age of the Old Woman of Beare? Every year on her birthday, her father slaughtered a beast and kept the horns in a pit. Then when the horns were counted 'twas easy to tell the number of her half-years. She lived to be nine hundred and seventy years of age. That was

a great age. How many horns was that, boy?
You're not long from school."

By the time I had calculated it and told
him, a few visitors had arrived and were
hanging up their caps on the pegs behind the
door. Now Johnny seemed to have forgotten
about the long cart, in his interest in the
visitors. I was hoping he would not remember
it for the rest of the evening. If he began to
talk about it to other people, they might
recognise, as I had, that it had not all happened in his imagination. The men were joking
him now, saying that he must run in the old
men's sack-race at the sports.

"To be sure I will," said Johnny. "But 'twill
take practice. You can't do a thing like that
without practice."

Several men offered themselves as trainers. Johnny accepted them all. He seemed to
have forgotten the contempt for sports which
he had so recently expressed to me. The
sports were going to be wonderful. There
were prizes for races of man and beast, and
for the tug-o'-war, and prizes for singing and
bagpiping and melodeon playing. As well as
these there would be currach races, and little
Patsy Ward's circus which was reported to be
on its way to Barrinish already, from Galway.

After a while, Tom and I sitting on the two hobs found ourselves being gazed at fixedly by two old men who were feeling the cold. At the same moment we both stood up and offered them our warm seats. They gave little cries of delight as if this were a great surprise to them, and skipped in agilely to sit down before we could change our minds. By degrees we moved towards the door and presently went outside. By this time the room was blue with pipe-smoke, so that no one missed us.

I took Tom out on the road away from listening walls, before telling him my story.

"That sounds like your Viking, all right," he said. "Unless it was someone moving a dead cow."

I had not thought of this. At first it seemed to me that the very simplicity of the explanation proved it to be right. But after a moment I said:

"No, Johnny saw those horns on a human head, I'm sure. Remember that he thought he would like to have some himself. Besides, who would put a dead cow on a cart and take her for a drive on the old road over the mountain?"

"Perhaps they wanted to bury her up there," Tom suggested.

"Then why did they chase Johnny away? There should be no secret about burying a cow. They did chase him away, so that he put curses on them, all the colours of the rainbow. And besides, no cow died in the island lately."

With us, the death of a cow is almost as great a tragedy as the death of a man. If such a misfortune had fallen on anyone, it would have been the talk of the island. Tom said:

"Whatever those people were up to, they wanted to keep it secret. Why didn't you ask Johnny who they were?"

"How could I?" I demanded indignantly. "I might as well have asked the cat. Johnny says what he wants to say and no more. 'Twas a miracle to get even that much talk out of him."

"Easy on," said Tom soothingly. "I was only thinking that it would be a good thing if he had said the names of the people driving the cart."

"Perhaps he didn't know them," I said. "I don't think that Johnny would curse a neighbour."

While we were talking we had wandered down on to the quay. The wind had risen during the evening. It seemed that the tailor's prophecy of another storm was going to come true. It was a westerly wind, clear and clean and wild. And very faintly on its breath I heard the song of the cave. It was so thin a sound still that it might have been only the whistling of the wind. I glanced sideways at Tom and saw that he had not noticed it. I pulled him to a standstill and made him listen. After a moment he said:

"That won't be a secret for much longer. At the next storm, your cave will be howling like a hyena."

A man had come up out of the hold of the lobster-boat and was watching us. He was a Breton, one of the three who worked on the boat and who had been coming here ever since I could remember. His name was Louan. He was a big, slow, gentle man who always wanted to talk about his wife and eight children at home in Brittany. He waved to us and called out in his careful English which nevertheless had an occasional word of French or Breton or Irish mixed up in it:

"Why don't you come down on to the bád? The others have gone out in the dinghy and I have no company."

At any other time we would have jumped at the chance. Above all things we loved sitting on the bunks in the crew's quarters,

listening to the Bretons' talk of their voyages
over the seven seas. It made no difference to
our enjoyment that we believed only half of
their stories. Now, however, we did not want
to leave the quay. From it we could see the
whole village, and a good piece of the road out
towards Mr Allen's house. I called out to
Louan:

"I'm watching out for my grandfather
coming home. We'll sit down here for a while
if it's all the same to you."

We sat on the edge of the quay and dangled
our legs over the deck of the *Saint Ronan*.
Louan sat down cross-legged on the deck and
got out his pipe. He looked up at us with calm
enjoyment through the smoke. Its scent mixed
rather pleasantly with the smell of lobsters
from the hold.

"This evening I am the watch-dog," he said.
"Tomorrow it will be my turn to enjoy myself.
There's our bold capitan gone off to visit Mr
Allen, and Michel and Abel gone this long
hour in the dinghy. No one comes to see me
except the seagulls, and I think they really
come to see the lobsters."

"Where have Michel and Abel gone?" I
asked without taking my eyes off the road.

"It's a queer thing," said Louan eagerly, "a

very queer thing. At home in Brittany we
have a strange kind of cave that is called in
French 'La Grotte qui Chante'. That would be
in English 'the cave that sings', I suppose.
They are all the same—a small cave outside
and inside a long, deep, sandy cave. When the
wind blows high and strong, it sings in and
out through the fingery stones between the
two caves. Once you have heard that song you
can never forget it. This evening we were
sitting here on the deck after supper, Michel
and Abel and I, and we heard a cave singing.
Twenty years we are coming to this áit, and
we never knew there was a grotte qui chante
near. So Michel and Abel got out the dinghy
and went off to find it. Listen!" He cocked his
head on one side and held up his pipe as if he
were pointing to the sound. "Can you hear it?
That high, sharp whistle like a seagull far
away? That is a singing cave. Can you hear
it?"

"Yes, yes indeed," we croaked in unison,
glad that our voices had come back to us.

Louan pulled at his pipe again and hitched
himself more comfortably together.

"But the queerest thing of all is that our
caves, when they opened up first, all had a
Viking inside!"

He looked at us triumphantly. I managed to say in a tone of vast surprise:

"A Viking!"

"Yes, indeed," said Louan. "A Viking with armour and weapons, sitting in a boat—"

This was too much for Tom. He burst out:

"Do you mean that *all* of these Vikings were the same, with helmets and horns and big black boats?"

Louan looked at him curiously. After a moment he said slowly:

"Yes, they did have helmets with horns, and their boats were black, though I had not said it. How do you know about those things?"

"There was a picture in our history-book at school," said Tom lamely.

"Ah, school," said Louan. "I would not have thought that you would have remembered so much from school." But he was laughing up at us now so that we could see he was satisfied with the answer. After a moment he went on:

"Yes, it is a strange thing that all the Vikings should be so much alike. In our part of Brittany we give a good reason for it. The story is that these old warriors were buried with their weapons and their boats so that if ever their country were in danger they could sail out and be ready to fight for their people.

It is a good story. It would be a fine thing if your country were in danger to have the best fighters out of the history-book there to help you. Just think of it—all those caves singing together, and the high seas covered with a fleet of Vikings sailing home. The only trouble is that it did not happen that way. The caves opened one by one after storms, and the Vikings went off to live in the museums." He sighed. "That is life, I suppose."

I hardly heard the last part, my head was so full of the wonderful story he had told. Now I could understand why my Viking had had the look of a man who is waiting for something. I longed to ask Louan if a game had been found with any of the Breton Vikings, but I knew that this would be madness. I said casually:

"We have a cave hereabouts which has always been called the Singing Cave. But we say it is because the seals go in there and sing before a storm."

"I never heard singing here before now," said Louan.

"Neither did I," said Tom.

"Seals are queer fellows," said Louan. "They often turn into men at the fall of night, they say, though I have never seen it myself. I know a man who landed on Deer Island once, late in the evening. He thought he would spend the night there, because there was a storm coming, so he made a bed of bracken for himself between two big rocks near the shore. The bracken on Deer Island is taller than a man. Have either of you ever been there?"

We said no, but that we were planning to go there some day and bring home one of the wild deer that roam the island, to eat.

"You leave those deer alone," said Louan fiercely. "Do you hear me? Don't you touch those deer."

Because he was so much excited, we promised hastily not to go to Deer Island at all, except perhaps to look at the deer and the giant bracken.

"What happened to the man who spent the night there?" I asked, to bring him back to a more soothing subject.

"Ah, yes. He made his bed, as I was saying, and when the sun went down he got in between the two rocks and lay there. But he could not sleep. The deer kept coming around to have a look at him, and the waves were big and noisy, and after a while the ticks in the bracken began to nip at him. So he lay until

the moon came up, and brightened the island
and the sea like broad white daylight. Then
he sat up, because the ticks were annoying
him, and he saw six seals come up out of the
sea. They shook the water off themselves and
crawled a piece up over the sand, and then
one by one they stood up straight and he saw
that every one of them was a man. You may
be sure that my friend stayed very quiet. The
seal-men sat in a ring on the sand and talked
to each other, and played a queer game with
stones. And all night long they sang strange
old songs that my friend had never heard
before. Maybe they were the songs that were
in fashion when those men were changed into
seals. Of course they would have no way of
learning new ones."

"Why didn't your friend go down and talk
to them, and find out all about them?" I said.
"He had no courage. I would have asked them
all kinds of questions, if I had been there."

"Would you now?" said Louan with interest.
"If you had been there and had gone down to
ask them questions, you'd have a fish-tail and
flippers and a big moustache this moment, for
you would have turned into a seal yourself.
That is why no one can learn anything about
them. If you talk to them you become one of

them, and then I suppose your curiosity is satisfied, all right."

"Do they turn into men every night?" Tom asked, though we only half believed this story of Louan's friend.

"It's said that it only happens at the full moon," said Louan, "and of course they must be sure to be near a cave, or a rock, or an island then, or they would be drowned. It is not a life that I would care for. It's said that they like to go into a ruined house, or an empty sheep-hut if they can find one. There are no buildings on Deer Island, so they had to spend the night sitting on the sand. In the morning they all became seals again and crawled back into the sea. So you see that sound we hear could not be seals' singing. They only sing by night."

He looked at us sharply as if he had guessed that we knew more than we were saying. Tom said feebly:

"There's no one that doesn't change his habits sometimes. I never heard that sound until this evening."

"Here comes the dinghy," said Louan comfortably, "so we'll know in a moment."

It came shooting into the little harbour, banging through the choppy sea as if it were propelled by an engine instead of by the two stout little Bretons who were rowing. It was the shortest boat I have ever seen, being barely long enough for the two men to sit one in front of the other on the thwarts. The oars were short and stumpy like the men who were handling them. The boat and the oars were painted a bright blue, a colour that we never use on boats, so that they looked very foreign to our eyes. As it came closer, Louan went over to the outer rail and shouted:

"Well, and how are the seals?"

Michel called back:

"They are well and send you their compliments, and hope you will join them soon!"

With a last pull they brought the boat alongside and skipped on board the *Saint Ronan*. "Well, what did you find?" Louan demanded impatiently. "Is it a *grotte qui chante*?"

"Yes, yes, just like ours. It sings even louder. We were inside. It was deafening. We think it is not long open. The stones are lying about the entrance. We only had matches so we could not see much."

"Was there a Viking?"

"No. It was quite empty. Perhaps the Viking has sailed off home to Denmark."

"Did you go right in to the back?"

"Yes, yes. Right inside. It was quite empty."

Now I saw that while we had been watching the approach of the dinghy, my grandfather and Mr Allen had strolled down the quay and were listening to Michel. Mr Allen had his pipe going, and he was sucking at it as contentedly as a baby at a bottle. But my grandfather looked as glum as I have ever seen him. It was clear that his visit to Mr Allen had brought him no comfort. Looking at him made me glum too, for I could guess all too well at what had happened. Mr Allen said easily:

"Who was looking for Vikings?"

"These two little heroes were," said Louan, pointing to his friends. "We heard a cave singing, as I was telling the boys, and Michel and Abel went in the dinghy to see if it would be like ours, with a Viking sitting, but now as you hear, they say it is empty."

"There could not be a Viking in it," said Mr Allen calmly. "The Vikings never came to this part of Ireland."

Without a trace of a smile he glanced at each of us in turn and then pulled long and thoughtfully at his pipe.

6

We Meet Patsy Ward and
Visit Johnny Gill

or hours, it seemed, we
stood there in a silly
dream and listened to
the slow, even discussion that followed. No
one seemed to notice that neither my grandfather nor either of us boys joined in. With
open mouths we heard Louan and his friends
talk of the queer things that are sometimes
found in caves. Louan repeated the whole
story of the six seal men who had landed on
Deer Island, and the others added stories of
seals wounded in the hunt who had turned
into men when they were at the point of
death. Presently they came back to telling
about their own singing caves at home.

They said it was a strange thing that we
should have here a cave of that name and
that when it opened itself up after a storm,

there was no Viking inside.

Watching Mr Allen placidly replying, it seemed to me that if there were any justice in the world, live toads should be hopping out of his mouth every moment, as happened to the liar in the story.

It was pitch dark and very cold before we moved. We were waiting for Mr Allen to let fall a careless word. He did not, not even when Big Dan Moloney came marching down the quay making a great clatter on the flags with his nailed boots. He jumped down on to the deck of the *Saint Ronan*, with a noise like a load of stones falling. Then he turned to glare around at our faces, dimly lit by the tired flame of the ship's lantern hanging on the cabin door.

" 'Tis a cold night for standing around talking," he said abruptly. "Them that have a good bed would do well to go there. Good night to you all."

And he marched into the cabin taking the lantern with him. We could hear him banging about inside and muttering to himself in bad temper.

"There is a fine example of Irish hospitality," said Louan comfortably, pulling at his pipe. The little glow from the tobacco showed an expression of quiet amusement around his mouth. "Now a Breton gentleman would never speak like that. He might get into his boat without speaking, yes. He might take the only light and leave you in the dark, yes. But he would never invite you to go home in so many words, not if he were on the point of falling asleep." He yawned widely, and then gave a little gentle laugh.

" 'Tis foreshown to me that we're not wanted here any longer," said Tom into my ear, in a beautiful imitation of old Luke Duffy's high-pitched whining voice.

The strange thing was that Mr Allen gave no sign of being offended. We knew from experience that he liked well-mannered people. Even his sour-hearted Sarah would have been afraid to drop an uncivil word in his presence. But now he just took my grandfather by the arm and turned gently about, and walked up the quay with us, and said good-bye at the cross as if nothing had happened. After he had gone we stood still for a moment and listened to the even, soft sound of his steps dying away on the night air as he started homewards.

Silently we walked as far as Tom's house. The half-door was shut and his father was peering over it, looking down the road for signs of Tom coming home.

"There you are," he said heartily. "I thought you were going to spend the night in the bushes with the birds."

With a word to me about meeting him in the morning, Tom went inside.

Then my grandfather said sadly:

"I'm afraid Mr Allen thinks we're terrible liars, Pat. 'Twas bad enough to have him tell me above in his own house that you had made up the whole story of the Viking. But when we came down the quay and heard you talking to Louan about Vikings and seals and singing caves—that must have seemed proof positive to him."

"How could it?" I said indignantly, but even as I said it I knew what the answer would be.

"Mr Allen thinks that Louan put the whole idea into your head with talk of Breton singing caves, and that you let on to have found a Viking in ours."

"But what about the game? Didn't you tell him you saw that yourself?"

"I did, God help me. But when I can't show it to him, how can he believe me?"

By the troubled tone of his voice I could see that he still had no suspicions of his friend. I thought of all the things that Mr Allen had told me, and that I had believed without proof. I had never asked him to show me a humming-bird, or a crocodile. I started indignantly to say some of this to my grandfather, but he looked so hurt that I could not go on. Almost in silence we walked home, and went to bed. More than once during the night I got up and went to the window to listen to the cave singing gently in the darkness. I knew well that in every house in the island dark figures would be showing in doorways tonight, every ear stretched to hear the unfamiliar sound which had become clearer when the day-time noises had died away. I knew too that each of those listeners would already have planned to get out his currach early and discover what was causing the sound. Every man of them loved a mystery. They would never rest until they had investigated this one.

In the morning, it happened just as I had imagined. Quite early, while the sea was still the colour of the inside of an oyster-shell, black specks began to appear on the satiny water, moving leisurely along the line of the shore towards the cliffs. Tom and I stood at the quay wall for a while and watched them.

Suddenly Tom turned impatiently.

"I've been counting the hours all night till we could go out to the cave," he said bitterly, "but we can't go now with all those curious people on their way there."

"There's not much to see anyway," I said shortly. "Come on away and meet Patsy Ward's circus."

Tom looked a little more cheerful.

"They were saying in our house that he spent last night at Rossaveel," he said. "He should be nearly here by now."

Patsy was an early starter, as we knew. He had to be. Always after his last night in a place, he and his wife and their nine children would take down the circus tent, and fold it on the huge cart that carried it, and pack all their belongings into their one caravan. Thus they would be ready to start on the road at five o'clock in the morning.

We captured an old white horse that belonged to Tom's father, and rode him along the coast road towards the bridge. This horse was a pensioner who had not worked for several years. He was not pleased to be forced into service again, and he did all he could to make us feel guilty at having upset his honourable retirement. He plodded along with his head down, smelling anxiously at the stones. He lifted each hoof tiredly as if it weighed a ton and with every step he contrived to slide about on the gravel to show how we were endangering his life by our callousness.

We did not mind how slow he was. There is a fine and unusual view of the countryside from a horse's back. For a while we rode with our heads turned downwards so that we could watch the quay, where the *Saint Ronan* still lay sleepily moored. Then when we came in sight of it, we watched Mr Allen's house. A quiet trickle of smoke came from its chimney. We could see Mr Allen himself moving peacefully around his garden, puffing calmly at his pipe. He waved to us as we passed slowly by. The horse took a fancy to turn into the shed, but we pulled his mane for him until he changed his mind and plodded down the road again.

Suddenly he stood stock still and quivered all over. His head came up and he shook his straggly old mane from side to side. Then he gave a long, tittering whinny, and stamped several times with one hoof.

We looked down towards the bridge and saw what he was laughing at. It was Patsy Ward's circus, just about to cross the bridge.

Though I had seen it several times before, I always felt the same rush of delight in its strangeness. Other circuses came to Barrinish from time to time, but none of them were in the least like Patsy's.

First came sixteen tiny ponies, harnessed in fours to a broad flat cart on which the tent lay in a great cone-shaped pile.

Then came Patsy, marching like a general in front of eight of his nine children, two abreast. Lastly came Mrs Ward driving the caravan with two more ponies which were accompanied by the family's dairy of six goats. Everything about the group was orderly, even to the way in which the goats had divided themselves so that three of them ran at either side of the caravan. One child always sat with Mrs Ward to keep her company while she drove.

Both Patsy and his wife were the smallest people I have ever seen. They were not midgets. Patsy was the size of a well-grown boy of twelve, and his wife was a little smaller. The children were stocky and well-built. Even the younger ones were as efficient and responsible as little men and women. Each had his own part of the business in his complete charge. One fed the ponies. One

bought the family's food from farms and shops
as they passed by. One milked the goats and
tended the kids that always travelled in a tea
chest in the back of the caravan until they
were fit for sale or for eating. One played the
fiddle to entertain the people waiting to go
into the circus; two provided accordion music
in the tent, in the intervals of the acts. One
had charge of little posters and handbills full
of information about the most stupendous
circus on earth, and this one also kept the
van painted and carried the water from the
nearest well when they were in camp. Of the
remaining two, one helped Patsy with train-
ing the ponies and selling the tickets, and the
other helped Mrs Ward with the family's
cooking and washing. They never quarrelled
with each other, and they never complained
of being tired or hungry. These facts alone
made them the wonder and the envy of every
boy in Connemara.

Their shows were crowded everywhere they
went, because they always finished up with a
play which was performed by the whole family.
Patsy used to compose the plays himself.
They were usually true stories of the recent
doings of people in other parts of Connemara.
The real name of the place and the names of

the people concerned would be given, so that the play was a way of spreading news from all over Connacht. You may be sure that any man who had fourpence to spend would not miss the chance of hearing how the fishing or the harvest was going in other places, how much wrack had been washed up, what matches were being made and who had died.

Patsy's information was always reliable. His memory was good, and he never forgot people's names and faces. He was pleased to see us waiting for him by the bridge. Even after the long march from Rossaveel, the whole family was stepping along firmly. They waved and called out to us as cheerfully as a little flight of jackdaws.

We felt too tall on the horse, so we got down and led him while we walked beside Patsy. As soon as he was over the bridge, he sniffed the air once or twice and said:

"Ah! It's grand to be back on an island. 'Tis a fine thing to smell the salty sea all around you. But I do like a little bridge to the mainland at the same time. I was born and bred on Horse's Island where there is but the one road, and in the stormy winter you couldn't go ashore only once in three months. I used to be walking up and down that road, dreaming of roads that go on and on over mountain and valley, over hill and hollow forever. Since those times, somehow I don't like to be prisoned on an island."

"You have plenty of roads to walk on now, Patsy," I said solemnly.

"I have, then," said Patsy. He expanded his little chest and swung his arms as heartily as if he were at the beginning instead of the end of his march. "I'm thinking 'twas living on Horse's Island gave me such a taste for them. 'Tis a terrible thing to have but the one road."

Presently we came to the little road that leads to our quay. We turned down there, and stopped at the wide flat grassy patch just above the harbour. One would think it was specially made to take a circus tent. All of the Wards began to scuttle about like ants, each at his own task. We helped them a little, but they did not really want us. After a few minutes Tom said:

"The men are all back from the Singing Cave, I'm thinking."

They were. The strand was black with currachs.

"I haven't seen the cave yet," said Tom.

"There's nothing to see," I said.

"I'd like to see it just the same," said Tom.

Michel waved to us from the deck of the *Saint Ronan* as we pushed off our currach. He was shifting lobster boxes with a great clatter, as if the boat were going to sea again soon. There was no sign of Big Dan nor of the other two. It was a clear, calm day with high, still clouds. A faint line, far out, showed where the sky met the sea. It was so quiet that we could hear the bows of the currach slipping gently through the water.

I should not have been surprised to have found one or two currachs still moored by the cave. It was quite deserted, however. From the outside one would have thought that there was nothing there to interest a visitor. We climbed over the broken stones, feeling our way in the dimness. Someone had left a candle-end, so that I could have taken Tom over every inch of the story of my find.

But the sandy floor was now all trampled over, as if a fair had been held in the cave. There was only one difference now between this and the many caves that we knew along the coast. That was the faint humming sound which even in this calm weather kept up a little accompaniment to our talk. Presently we left it and rowed back silently to the quay.

We knew that we would not be able to

meet again until late in the evening. We had spent an idle morning, and after dinner there would be turf to carry, and cows to be moved to a new pasture, and sea-weed for manure to be brought up from the shore, and a dozen other things just as important.

At dinner-time I learned from my grandfather that the Singing Cave was the talk of the island. It seemed to me that he had already despaired of ever hearing what had become of the Viking. I answered him shortly enough, as if I were beaten too, for I did not want to tell him yet that I had not given up hope. I knew that he would disapprove of the spying that Tom and I had done yesterday, and which we intended to pursue further this evening.

On such a good day for outdoor work, I guessed that the men would be tired, and ready for a long gossip in our kitchen in the evening. I made sure to be gone by the time the first one would arrive, lest the laws of hospitality might keep me glued to my stool by the fire until after midnight. Indeed I was just two fields away when I glanced back and saw Lord Folan on his way to our door.

Tom was waiting for me up at the old stone stable behind his own house. Once, in the bad old times, long before Tom was born, this had been the family house. The new one was lower down the hill, sheltered and snug, and the Joyces' horse was left in possession of the old house with the winds of winter whistling through the gaping windows to keep him company.

Just by the stable, the old road over the mountain straggled along until it became a marshy track. And up there was Johnny Gill's house. We had decided to visit Johnny and try to make him talk a little more about what he had seen.

Even on a fine spring evening, that was a dismal road. The wind cried over the sedgy bog and was answered by the wild whistles of those lonesome birds that lived up there. As darkness fell, the only light came from the tiny window of Johnny's kitchen. It was a candle's light, for Johnny could never be taught how to manage a lamp, and its weak flickering made me feel as if the whole world had grown small and far away. I began to remember that this was the road that the famine funerals used to take, and that on a dark night you might see four silent earnest men of a hundred years ago, solemnly playing cards on a flat stone by the roadside. If you saw that sight, they said, you would not live to see the year's end.

I was walking as close to Tom as I could without letting him suspect what horrid thoughts were pounding through my head. We were quite near to Johnny's house now. At one side of the road was a half-hearted grass-grown wall which had once enclosed a meadow. Suddenly Tom seized my arm and almost threw me over the wall. I made no sound. We lay there, hard against the stones, knee-deep in a boggy drain, and listened.

In a moment I heard what Tom had heard. Someone was walking fast and lightly, along the road after us. Still there was a kind of small hesitation in the step, as if the person were pressed for breath.

Very cautiously, we lifted our heads until we could look over the wall. The moon was not yet up, but there was a brightness in the sky that showed it was not far away. Gradually bushes and rocks were beginning to show black against the grey bog.

"Down!" said Tom's voice in my ear. "Here he comes. It's Mr Allen."

Through a little hole in the wall we watched him by turns until he had gone past. It was Mr Allen, sure enough, hurrying along as if he were being hunted. It was very strange to see this, for I had never before known him to be in a hurry. It was one of his principles that a wise man never hurries. I had tried more than once in private to copy his slow, smooth, dignified gait and his measured, philosophical pronouncements, but I had had to decide that the style did not suit me. Besides, the other boys would never have allowed it.

"He's going to visit Johnny Gill too," I said after a moment. "If we had been ten minutes earlier, he would have found us there."

In the brightening moonlight, we watched him follow the wriggling flagged path to Johnny's door. He seemed now to move even more quietly, and as he approached the house, even at that distance the thought came to me suddenly that he looked like a thief. We moved a little closer, keeping under the shadow of the wall. We did not hear him knock, though he stayed by the door for several minutes.

"It looks like Johnny won't let him in," I said presently. "He's going away again."

Five minutes later we were slithering up to Johnny's house like a couple of snakes. We peered in through the window first. Johnny was there, all right, sitting at the head of the table singing the ballad of "Blooming Caroline from Edinburgh town", and conducting himself solemnly with his right hand. His voice had a queer sweetness in it, in spite of a rasping wheeze that made it sound a little like a mouth-organ. I have heard that the Chinese sing in this way. We could hear every word quite clearly from outside. Once or twice he stopped and admonished himself for going too fast or too slowly, and ordered himself to go back to the beginning and start all over again.

"Practice makes perfect," he said firmly. "Practice is necessary. If you don't practice, Johnny Gill, you'll never make a singer!"

We were doubled up with laughter outside the window, but he was far too busy to hear us. We thought at first that this was why he had not heard Mr Allen either. But when we went to the door, we found that the hasp had been put across, and a smooth peg slipped into the ring. In this way Johnny was firmly imprisoned in the house. There was only one door, and the windows were too small for him to be able to get through even if he were to think of it.

7

We Set Sail in the *Saint Ronan*

 ook at that for villainy!"
Tom whispered indig-
nantly. He lifted the peg
out and put it in his pocket. "If the house
were to go on fire tonight, Johnny would
never get out of it alive."

"I suppose he didn't think of that," I said
lamely.

I had been very much attached to Mr Allen
and now it hurt me to find still more proof
against him. I could see, of course, that he
would not have troubled to lock Johnny in if
he had not known something of the long cart
on which Johnny said he had seen the devil's
horns.

We talked about this in whispers as we
followed along the way that Mr Allen had
gone. Since Johnny had been locked in, it

looked as if something were going to happen tonight. We were able to move fast, because now the road was quite overgrown with grass on which our footsteps made no sound.

Still it was twenty minutes before we caught sight of Mr Allen again. He was going more slowly now, as if he were tired, though we had crossed over the ridge of the island and were on our way downhill. Away down below us was the empty townland called Cashel. We could see the sea again, and well back from it, in the middle of the only patch of good flat land on the island, there was a dark clump of trees. Somewhere among them was the tumbledown half-ruin that was Mr Allen's old home.

"That's where he's going, of course," said Tom. "We should have thought of it long ago."

"He doesn't sleep well," I said. "I remember now that he walks there sometimes at night, when he's restless. He told us that once."

Tom made no reply, and I was silent. It certainly was ridiculous that I should now begin to make excuses for Mr Allen, since I had so firmly accused him to Tom a short time ago. That had been easy when I was working out a theory as if it were a sum in arithmetic. But now that I saw Mr Allen before my eyes, all kinds of doubts began to creep into my mind. If I had been alone, I might have turned back even now, but I could see that Tom was not going to be put off so easily.

All down the long road we followed him, darting from shadow to shadow of the rare bushes that grew by the roadside. Mr Allen looked back many times so that it seemed he must sooner or later see us flitting across. But we were lucky, or else his sight was not good, for he always continued on his way as if he were quite sure that he was not observed.

In this way we saw him reach the edge of the trees. We knew that here was an ancient stone arch, which was the entrance to the avenue of the house. We gave him time to walk a little way along the avenue, and then we came ourselves as far as the arch.

There was no gate. It had been a huge wrought-iron one, but it had been taken away long ago, when it had become dangerously rickety and might have fallen on someone. We peered into the darkness and suddenly saw him, crossing a shaft of moonlight. We waited a little while, sitting with our backs to the stone. I could hear Tom whistling under his breath the tune of "Blooming Caroline", but we did not talk.

Presently Tom stood up and said:

"He must be at the house by now."

We left the avenue then and moved among the trees, so that in a little while we came out by the side of the house. Now the moon shone strong and clear, so that the house seemed to float in a lake of soft, pale light. The door was ajar on a black cavern. A candle fluttered like a will-o'-the-wisp from the dusty window beside it. It was all so quiet that a family of foxes, father, mother, and four very young cubs, were tumbling and playing on the short grass before the door, where once there had been a gravel sweep. A blackbird shrieked suddenly from a bush, disturbed by our movements.

"If I had that fellow, I'd wring his neck," said Tom's voice in my ear.

The foxes scattered as we ran across the patch of open moonlight to reach the window. Crouched against the house wall, we paused for a moment and then lifted our heads boldly at the same moment and took a long look into the room.

Mr Allen was there, standing in the middle of the bare floor holding a candle in his hand. At his feet was a long wooden chest, like a sea-chest but bigger, and very much battered. He was looking down into it with an expression of mild annoyance. While we watched, he moved a step or two away from the chest and back again, impatiently. We scarcely had time to wonder what he was doing when another candle-flame brightened in the doorway, and Big Dan Moloney walked into the room. I could not forbear from giving a little shriek of amazement, for on his head was my Viking's helmet.

Tom whispered hotly into my ear to be still. Mr Allen's voice came clearly through the broken window.

"Take that thing off your head," he said querulously. "It makes me nervous."

"And how else would I carry it?" Big Dan demanded. "I have a candle in one hand and this old sword in the other, and still I'm supposed to be able to carry the hat. The world knows that the best way to carry a hat is to wear it."

"Stop calling it a hat," said Mr Allen. "It's a helmet. Now put those things down carefully."

"You're a terrible man for giving orders," Big Dan grumbled.

But he did as he was told, for we heard the

soft clatter of the sword on the boards as we crouched down again out of sight. They argued then about the best way to pack the sword and the helmet into the box. Big Dan said firmly:

"The best way to carry a hat is to wear it. Put it on his head, I tell you."

So then I knew for certain that my Viking was in the box.

I remember that I was astonished to hear anyone speak to Mr Allen with such small respect. But the last trace of my pity for him was gone now. The desolation of his house gave me the shivers, and I began to wonder for the first time whether it had been misfortune or wickedness that had brought it to ruin.

Now suddenly we became afraid of being discovered hidden under the window like thieves. We waited for no more. A thin cloud had covered the moon, but we dared not cross the open grass again lest either of the men might glance outside and see us. Instead we kept to the house wall until we could skip around the corner and so into the trees.

Still we did not stop. Tom led the way, across a low bank and down a grassy laneway, until we came to the ruin of a tiny stone cottage. Its walls stood four-square, but the thatched roof had fallen in, and tall grass grew where the earthen floor had been. This cottage had once belonged to a family called Conneeley, who had gone to America in the bad times, and had made money in the building business. Their descendants were millionaires in Chicago, I had been told, but I am not sure if this was true.

From the cottage we could see the stone archway that led on to the avenue. We sat just inside the empty doorway and settled down to watch. Though we knew that we were safe now, still for the first minutes we did not dare to speak. Then I said:

"I suppose the Viking is so old that Mr Allen forgets he was ever a man at all."

"Mr Allen is cold-hearted," said Tom. "It seems to me he cares for nothing except books, and what the other scholars will say if they find out that he was wrong in what he wrote about the Vikings. Aunt Minnie always says: 'Never lay down the law about anything, for you'll only look foolish when someone is able to contradict you.'"

"It's a pity Mr Allen didn't meet your Aunt Minnie when he was young," said I, "and he might never have written about the Vikings at all."

"It's too late to wish for that now," Tom said. "Tonight that Viking will sail for Brittany, I'm thinking, and if we ever want to see him again, you and I must go with him."

We paused for a long time to think about this. At last I said:

"Can we not steal him before they get him to the boat?"

"We can try, I suppose, but you'll see that they will be very careful not to leave him. We can't snatch him and run. And we can't have a fight without help."

"We should tell Lord Folan and my grandfather and all the men about it," I said. "They would make Mr Allen open the box and show what is in it before letting him put it on board the *Saint Ronan*."

"Lord Folan and the rest of them will be in their beds long before that box gets to the quay," said Tom. "And even if they were not, you know that none of the men would force Mr Allen to open it. We'd have a hard time persuading them that he would do anything wrong."

"Patsy Ward would help us, then."

"He would, but Patsy is too small, Patsy and his whole family would hardly make the weight of two men if it came to a fight."

"I suppose the board and all the little wolves' heads are in the box too," I said sadly.

Only for that game, I believe I would have let the Viking sail to the world's end. But if we let the game go now without a struggle, I knew that the thought of it would gnaw me as long as I drew breath.

We sat there for a long time, slowly talking over what was to be done. It was cold, and the damp began to seep into our clothes. More than an hour passed before we heard the soft sound of a horse's hooves on the avenue, and the quiet rumble of a well-oiled cart. We were waiting by the archway as they came through. It was a long cart, as Johnny had said, of a kind that our people never use. But I had seen it before, in the cart-shed of the old house when I had come to explore only last year. Then it had been heavy with cobwebs and dust, and one of its wheels had been lying on the floor for so long that the mice had nested between the spokes. Mr Allen must have made Big Dan put it together quickly, for he would not have wished to make his neighbours curious by borrowing a cart.

When they were just outside the gate, a

trace broke. Pressed flat against the archway, we heard Big Dan exclaim:

"More delays! Why couldn't you get a decent cart? This one was in the Ark, by the looks of it. And the old horse—we're lucky if we don't have to carry him before we reach the quay. In two shakes I'd leave you here to get on with your own blackguarding, so I would!"

But we heard him stamping about and cursing quietly as he mended the trace. Mr Allen stood by and made no attempt to help.

"What I am doing is not dishonest," he said coldly. "I know that the Vikings never came to these islands—"

Big Dan interrupted him with a derisive laugh.

"This horny man here is no Irishman, I'd swear. He looks to me uncommon like the lads that came over to fight the battle of Clontarf in 1014. Not that I was there, then, I'll be the first to admit, but I've seen their pictures so often that I'd know one of them boiled."

And he chuckled heartily again. Mr Allen said, in a flat contemptuous voice, full of anger:

"You know nothing of these things. But if your conscience troubles you before you get to

Kerronan, you will perhaps remember that you have not yet been paid."

"Conscience!" Big Dan was astonished. "If I never did worse than shift an old bag-o'-bones from one cave to another, I'd have good hopes of heaven. Box-o'-bones, I should say. There now, that will hold for a while." He rattled the trace once or twice to make sure that it would not fall apart again. "Now if we can get Methuselah to move, we can be off."

We could hear him thumping the horse, and then they moved slowly on again.

After a moment Tom whispered:

"That's our old white horse they have. No wonder he was tired this morning. I suppose they had him last night too."

We gave them a little start and then we began to follow them at a distance. We dared not stay on the road this time, because of Big Dan. It had been easy following Mr Allen, for he had a kind of innocence about him in spite of what he was doing. But Big Dan was as alert and sly as a weasel. Our whole plan would fail if he were to become suspicious of us now.

So we made our way through the bog, moving delicately from one to another of the little patches of firm ground. A dozen times we found ourselves marooned, and then we had to stop and plan our course as carefully as if we were at sea, lest we might sink into one of the black bog-holes that seemed to lie in wait for us on every side. Without the moonlight we should certainly have been lost. Its pale gleam on the water more than once gave us warning of danger.

Below Johnny Gill's house, the fields began again. Now that we were sure that the cart was going straight to our quay, we went faster and presently we passed it at one side and left it behind us. As we went down, we could see that the houses along the curve of Norseman's Bay were dark. Only two lights showed. One was from the open door of my grandfather's house, where I knew he would be sitting alone in the kitchen waiting for me. The other was from the tiny window of Patsy Ward's caravan.

Patsy was sitting on the wooden step that led up to his little front door when we arrived. The air was sweet with the smoke of his pipe. He did not seem surprised to see us when we slipped out of the darkness. He just gave a quick pull at his pipe and said:

"Good night, boys. Late ye're out."

"Good night, Patsy. Has anyone been

looking for us?"

"Sorro' one." He chuckled. "Ye're not so valuable as ye think. I'm here about the place all evening, putting up the tent first and then doing a few tricks with the ponies. Only now I said I'd have an old draw on the pipe before going to bed."

"Listen, Patsy. They will be looking for us. But we're going off on the *Saint Ronan*. She's sailing tonight."

He cocked an eye towards where she lay at the wall high on the full tide.

"She's sailing, sure enough," he said. "She's all shipshape and ready. The lobsters are fighting like cats below in the hold. The men are only waiting for Big Dan, they told me, and they'll be off on the half tide."

"Where are the men now?"

"Having a sleep, I'm thinking. Louan was up here an hour ago and he said he'd sleep while he had the chance. He was grumbling that they were going off in the dead of night, instead of waiting for the morning's light like Christians. He asked Big Dan what hurry was on him, and Big Dan nearly knocked him into the tide, so he didn't ask again. Sailoring is a hard life, I'm telling you." He looked at us sharply. "What's taking ye sailing at this hour of the night?"

We made him swear to keep our secret before we would tell him anything.

"Don't ye know well I'm as full as a tick with secrets," he said reproachfully, "and I don't tell no one."

So we told him the story of the Viking, and of how we were going to go with him on the boat and try to get him back.

"He's travelling along down the mountain now, with Mr Allen and Big Dan," I said. "They're going to Kerronan. All we want is for you to tell my grandfather where we're gone, and ask him to take out the hooker in the morning and come after us and bring us home."

Patsy agreed to do this. He had heard about the Singing Cave from the men who had strolled down in the evening to watch him put up the tent. He had not heard the song of the cave, he said, because the evening was so calm. He became very excited about the story of the Viking.

"Man, won't it make a great play! I'll make a bargain with ye, boys. In return for helping ye now, ye won't let anyone else make a play of that story until I have done it first."

He gave a little high laugh, like a cock's

crow, at the idea of it. We promised at once, of course. This was easy, because Patsy was the only man who made plays in the whole of Connacht, so far as we knew.

"Of course I'll wait for the end of the story," he said earnestly. "We don't know for certain what the end is going to be."

You may be sure that we did not like the sound of that. Patsy came with us down to the quay. There was no sound there, except the gentle rub of the *Saint Ronan* against the cut-stone wall, and the quiet little wash of the waves on the breakwater. We listened for a moment to the silence, until we began to hear the cry of the curlews away off in the bog, and the busy scutter of the stream that runs down on to the beach above the quay, three hundred yards away. It seemed to me that my ears grew big with listening, so that I could almost hear the hens turning in their sleep on their perches in the nearest farmyard. Then, far off, we heard the rumble of the cart coming down the mountain.

It was our last chance to turn back. The thought ran into my mind even while we boarded the *Saint Ronan* as quietly as if we were taking eggs from under a hen. Still she rocked a very little, so that we stopped dead and glanced uneasily towards the forecastle, expecting a head to pop suspiciously out. We knew that we could wait no longer, because soon the noise of the cart would arouse the men. We glanced back once towards Patsy, who looked not much bigger than a bollard as he stood on the quay. Then one after the other we slid down the companionway into the hold.

It was pitch-dark down there, except for a faint luminous square where the sea shone through the grid. The black shapes of the lobsters crossed and re-crossed it tiredly, perhaps because they had been fighting, as Patsy had said. We huddled close together on the narrow footway that ran around the tank.

It seemed an age before we heard the dull thump of sea-boots on the deck overhead. There was very little talk. Once Louan laughed short and sourly, when he realised, I suppose, that his captain was putting to sea in the dead of night because he was engaged in something shady. It was a tiny ship, and the sounds travelled into every corner of it. We heard the men carry the box into Big Dan's cabin and place it carefully on the floor. Big Dan's voice came hoarsely, giving directions about where it should lie. Presently they all stumped out on to the deck again.

A moment later they cast off. The water began to chuckle through the lobsters' grid. Then a gentle swing of the little ship told us that we had left the quay.

8

The Voyage to Kerronan

or hours we dared not move. As soon as we were under way, we found that on our narrow perch we were not very much better off than if we had been down with the lobsters in the tank. The *Saint Ronan* had been built for tough, wiry men who did not mind a pitch here and a roll there when they went to sea. Now we found that she bucked and reared like a young horse as soon as she got outside the harbour. Every one of her capers sent a great fountain of salt water climbing to the ceiling of our refuge. Soon we were as wet as herrings. It was not that we minded this for its own sake, but it made our ledge slippery, so that we were in momently danger of falling into the tank. If we had sat down, we might perhaps

have been steadier. But then our legs would
have had to dangle into the water, and we
knew from experience how the lobsters would
have relished our bare toes.

To begin with, we had had some idea that
we might be able to travel all the way to
Brittany in secret, and in secret follow Big
Dan ashore, and watch while he brought the
Viking to the other cave of which he had
spoken. But when we had been a little time in
the hold our hearts began to fail us. The
horrible darkness and the fishy stench of the
lobsters sucked away at our spirits, and what
was left of them was utterly banished by
hunger.

We were astonished now to think that we
had forgotten to bring food. When we went
out for a day's fishing, we would as soon have
left the currach's oars behind as our little
canvas bag full of bread and butter and eggs.
Even to think of it made us shiver with
desolation.

We knew when the dawn came, because
the colour of the sea's floor changed slowly to
a lighter green. Tom said:

"Soon 'twill be safe for us to go on deck.
The boat can't turn back now. Big Dan would
be afraid. The people would all be down to

ask why he was back so soon."

"He could say 'twas to bring us home," said I, though my heart had given a great leap at the idea of escaping from the hold.

But Tom said that Big Dan would be afraid that the box would be discovered while he was at the quay, and that he would never be paid by Mr Allen after all.

"Whatever happens, we must soon come out of here." He paused for a long time. "I wish we could eat some of the lobsters."

"I'm mighty glad we can't," I said. "I don't believe there would be any comfort in them."

Somewhere above our heads, not far away, one of the men began to sing softly. With longing we imagined the scene on the sunny deck, the lilting roll of the ship, the high-flying white clouds, the shining dancing sea. Then with a crash the hatch cover was thrown back, and on the top step of the companion ladder a huge boot appeared, lit up in a shaft of sunlight.

It paused there. We shrank as flat as the wall. Though we had just been talking of showing ourselves on deck, the sight of that boot filled me with terror, so that to this day I can see its curved toe and a thick ugly wrinkle by the ankle. The singing stopped.

Immediately we heard Big Dan's voice in a kind of snarl:

"Where would you be going, Louan?"

Louan answered with exaggerated cheerfulness as if he were humouring a cross dog:

"I'm just going down to have a look at the lobsters. A while before we left they were at each other's throats. I want to be sure they have no claws missing. The claws are the most delicate part."

"I'd as soon eat a mouthful of sea-weed," said Big Dan. "If there are any claws off, mind you stitch them on again!"

Louan laughed politely, as I suppose a sailor must always laugh at his captain's jokes. Then he began to climb step by step down the ladder, as awkward in his sea-boots as a swan on dry land.

At the foot of the ladder he paused, and peered about like a bat to accustom himself to the darkness. Then he began to walk carefully all around the tank, gazing deep into the water at the little silhouetted monsters that were washed about helplessly now by the movements of the ship. We knew that it was no use trying to move away ahead of him. Still we were afraid to call him and warn him of our presence, lest our voices might be heard on deck.

He was so intent on his purpose that he was almost upon us before he noticed us. He saw our bare feet first, ghostly grey now in the fringes of the sunlight that came down the companion way. We watched him follow slowly upwards until he was staring at our faces. We stared back, waiting from second to second for him to shout in surprise or anger. But he made no sound. His teeth gleamed in a smile and his eyes shone round with amusement. I could feel Tom's body quiveringly pressed against my arm. Then Louan leaned forward and said softly, so close to my ear that his breath tickled.

"Wait a little longer. I will come for you soon."

I gave no sign that I had heard, and he did not wait for it. Immediately he shuffled back by the way that he had come and presently clumped up the ladder again on to the deck. We heard Big Dan call out:

"Ha, Louan! Are the lobsters all fresh and well?"

"They're dancing minuets," said Louan comfortably.

Then he dropped the hatch cover into place and we were plunged into darkness again.

Now everything had changed, since we knew Louan would not betray us. Even the lobsters seemed more friendly and their smell almost sweet, so that the last part of our time in the hold was more easily endured than the first. Now that he had gone, I wished that I had asked Louan to bring us some food.

When he came again, he had thought of it himself. This time he came quietly, stealing down the companion-way like an eel slipping over a waterfall, and no voice followed him. He glanced around sharply in the gloom until he found us, and then came sidling along the ledge. He had a great fishy lump of soda-bread in each pocket. As we bit off huge, un-mannerly mouthfuls, the crumbs fell softly into the tank and the lobsters snapped at them. Louan said:

"Our brave capitan has gone to sleep. He was tired, poor fellow, because he got little sleep last night. I've told Michel and Abel that you are here. You can come along to our place now and we'll have some talk."

"We could do with a sleep ourselves," said Tom.

"Yes, yes, in our bunks. And we'll give you more food. Now come, very quietly, because we must not disturb the good capitan's sleep."

We went up that ladder and along the deck
as silently as planing seagulls. Up there the
air was just as sweet as we had imagined. We
had time only for two great breaths of it when
we were through the forecastle door and down
the ladder into the crew's quarters.

It was far better there than in the hold.
There were port-holes to let in the light, and
Michel and Abel, lying on their bunks, were
more welcome company by far than the lobsters had been. They lifted their heads and
looked at us with delight. They explained
that it was not often they had such enter-
tainment at sea. Michel asked why we had
come with them.

"We don't mean that you are not welcome,"
Abel said carefully.

"We want to see the world," said I.

"A very good reason," said Louan solemnly.
"The world is at Kerronan, and you'll certainly
see it there."

"Do your people know where you are?"
asked Abel, who had a more cautious nature
than the other two.

"We left a message," said Tom.

This satisfied them. They got out food for
us, more bread, and a light red wine, and
some very nasty shellfish that they reckoned

a great delicacy. They showed us how to pick these out of their hiding with a pin. We became quite clever at it.

Soon the men got off their bunks and made us lie down. Almost at once I fell into a heavy sleep.

I awoke to hear seagulls crying and the rumble of cart-wheels quite close. I sprang up, to dance from one porthole to another. I could see by the sun that it was evening. We were moored to a long stone quay, in a little land-locked harbour. All around were great green sloping hills, with clumps of trees and grazing cattle and sheep. Far in, there was a little town, with houses built almost over-hanging the water. High above it the ruins of a huge stone building looked down on the harbour.

Tom was still asleep, rolled over his head in his blankets. I shook him gently, for I did not want him to wake with a shout.

"We're in Kerronan," I whispered. "We must have been asleep for a few days. Louan and the others—they had a sleeping powder in the wine, I suppose."

In one great bound, Tom was off the bunk. As frantically as I had done, he darted from porthole to porthole, but after a glance or two

I saw him turn towards me with one eyebrow lifted in a way I knew well.

"This is Ireland still, Pat," he said softly. "Look at the big green hills. Look at the cows and sheep. If this were Brittany all those hills would be cut up into little flower-gardens, and vegetable-gardens. There would be houses all over them, with fruit trees in front. There would be dozens of men on this quay, boxing fish and shouting their heads off."

It was easy to see now that he was right. I could hardly take my eyes off those hills, now that I knew they belonged to my own country. I had never seen their like before. In Connemara the hills are brown with sedge and purple with heather and white with rocks. Our black cows are very clever at finding the scarce patches of grass that grow in between. If we have big grass hills, it is usually because there is sand beneath, with rabbits and weasels chasing each other in endless tunnels. By the length of the grass here and by its rich green colour, you could tell at once that it grew on good brown earth.

We could hear sounds above our heads, of feet tramping and wood scraping on wood, and voices calling out, high and clear as bird-calls on the light evening air. When the cart-

wheels rumbled again I was sure that my
Viking was being carried away. I started
towards the companion ladder. A moment
later Tom had me by the tail of my jersey.

"Where are you going?"

"I won't let him get away, I tell you, I
won't, while there's breath in me. Let me go!"

It was a good thing that Louan appeared
just then, or we might have been discovered
by Big Dan scuffling all over the cabin. Tom
let go of my jersey at once. Louan did not
speak until he had shut the door carefully.
Then he said in a low voice:

"You have well slept?"

We nodded.

"That is good. Now you are hungry again.
I will get out more food."

While he rummaged placidly for bread and
goat's milk cheese, I said:

"Where are we? What is happening here?"

"We are in Kinsale harbour," said Louan
calmly. "Our brave capitan had just bought
some lobsters and a few boxes of salmon.
We're sailing again in an hour's time. You
must stay quietly here until tomorrow, and
then perhaps we can arrange a little walk for
you."

"Does Big Dan never come down here?"

Tom asked as we began to eat.

"Hardly ever. And I'm certain that he will not come down tonight. The *Santa Teresa* from Vigo is moored right here beside us. That old trawler—she stinks of fish!" He wrinkled his nose, as if the *Saint Ronan* did not stink of fish too. "The capitain of the *Santa Teresa* has red wine, and he is entertaining our capitain in Spanish style with it. They have prawns too. I saw them. They did not ask me if I would like a prawn. And I would like a prawn, I tell you, I would like a prawn."

He stayed with us until it was time for him to go on deck and salvage his brave capitain, as he always called him, from the *Santa Teresa*. We dared not move. Through the tiny portholes we watched the darkness falling over that quiet harbour, which I think must be the most beautiful place in the whole world. Lights came up in the little town and in lonely cottages on the hill-tops. The dark green hills, reflected in the smooth water, turned slowly darker until they were inky black and speckled with stars. Then the moon came out, smoothly sailing, and laid a broad gold path across the sea.

We heard Louan helping the captain on

board. He was carolling a Spanish song at the top of his voice, repeating over and over one line that took his fancy:

"*Ay, la mujer es bonita!*"

"The prawns have gone to his head," said Tom solemnly.

His three sailors got him into his cabin, with promises that they would look after the ship. He must have fallen asleep at once, for we heard no more from him.

They cast off soon after that, with little songs to help them, very like our own songs. As soon as the *Saint Ronan* was a few feet away from the quay, we came up on deck. It was a joy to breathe clean sea air again, to run and jump along the deck as if we had been paralysed and had suddenly recovered the use of our limbs. At last I went to stand by Louan. He was steering confidently across the track of the moon and out through the harbour's mouth, which was guarded by two ancient stone forts.

"We come here very often," he said. "I know my way through this harbour as well as I know the path to my own front door."

"Where is your house, Louan?" I asked.

"In the Square of Kerronan," he said and laughed with delight at the thought of seeing it again soon. "Ah, Kerronan! That is a place! My eldest son Ronan is about the same age as you. This year he goes out with the sardine fishers. Next year he will come to sea with me."

Outside the harbour, a huge lighthouse sent a slow majestic beam sweeping across the sea like another moon.

"That is the Old Head of Kinsale," said Louan. "Many a dirty night, when I was working on the Spanish trawlers, we came in here and you could hardly see that light for spray."

For most of the night, we could not bring ourselves to go below again. One by one the lighthouses dropped away, until we were alone on a huge empty sea that never changed and still seemed always different. Towards morning, when the dawn winds blew cold, we became drowsy again and went down to sleep. I awoke suddenly in the broad daylight to find Big Dan's face glaring, four inches from my nose.

I lay quite still and looked back at him. I could not move. Big Dan's eyes were rimmed with red. His mouth was turned down in a snarl, so that I could have counted his broken teeth. His breath was hot with red wine. It was like being glared at by a wolf. My arms lay helplessly by my sides, though I longed to push him away from me with all my strength.

When he saw that I was wide awake, he withdrew a little.

"Passengers!" he said softly, with a fearful smile. "Two of them! Another one over there, sleeping like a baby!" He stepped aside so that I could see Tom, who now began to stretch and roll before waking up. "Excuse me for disturbing you, sir! And what the devil are you doing on my ship without an invitation?"

The last question was a sudden roar that sent Tom springing into the air. I took the opportunity of slipping off my bunk and over to the ladder.

"We just wanted to see—to see the world, sir," I said.

"You won't see much of the world from the deck of my ship," said Big Dan. "And I'll make full sure that you don't put a foot ashore. Did you bring any money with you?"

"No." I was astonished, for we never would have thought of bringing money to sea with us.

"Then you must work your passage. That's the law at sea. Up on deck now, both of you, and I'll find something useful for you to do.

An idle mind is the devil's workshop."

He was in such a hurry to plague us that he ran ahead calling out as he went:

"Abel, Abel! Buckets! Hot water! Brushes! This ship will be a credit to us when we reach Kerronan! I have found two mermaids to scrub for us!"

Louan was sitting in the moving shadow of the cabin, expertly darning one of his own red socks. He looked up quickly. He stuffed the sock into his pocket and stood up.

"Abel will not get buckets, and hot water, and brushes," he said.

"Why?" Big Dan demanded. "Is he sick! Abel! Abel! Are you sick or well?"

Abel poked his head cautiously around the door of the tiny galley amidships, where he was already cooking dinner. He looked miserably from Louan to Big Dan, but he said nothing.

"Abel is quite well," said Louan firmly. "But these boys are not going to scrub our decks."

"But they have brought no money. I will not have two young thieves walking on to my ship and sailing off to see the world without paying a penny for it. Buckets! Water! They are going to scrub!"

"They are not," said Louan, and he took another step forward, threateningly.

"This is mutiny," said Big Dan.

He lowered his head like a bull about to charge, and glared upwards through his eyelashes.

Louan shrugged.

"You can't have a mutiny on a ship as small as this," he said with contempt.

"She is the finest ship in the lobster trade," said Big Dan hotly.

"That may be," said Louan. "She will not long be in the lobster trade if you do not treat our guests with more care. I am not an Irishman, but I know Connemara better than you do. If you put those boys to scrub our decks, not a man in Connemara will ever sell us a gliomach again."

Though I knew that our people would be angry, I was not as sure as Louan was that they would support us with such determination. Big Dan was looking at us now with a little more respect, mixed obviously with disappointment at being cheated of his revenge. Then, on a sudden his eyes grew round and sparkled as a new idea struck him.

"Very well," he said softly. "Since you're so fond of them, we'll let them travel like gentlemen. And when we get into Kerronan, since you are so fond of them, you can sit here and chat with them as long as we are in port!"

At this, of course, we offered to scrub the decks, but Big Dan would not have it. Our relations might take offence if we were put to work, he said, and refuse to sell him lobsters. He said he hoped that we would enjoy our little trip, and that there was quite a good view of Kerronan from the quays. Then he stumped off into his cabin, mighty pleased with himself. We could hear him chuckling like a hen, all alone in there, for a long time afterwards.

9

A Party

or the rest of the journey we hardly dared to speak to the men. Louan sat and darned, and fetched a huge shivering sigh from time to time. Abel and Michel wagged their heads and glared at us, and would not even allow us the comfort of helping them at their work. It was a day of glorious sun, with high-sailing clouds and friendly wind of the kind that is sent to delight all sailors. But we could not take any pleasure in it now, being burdened as we were with the guilt of keeping Louan from his beloved family.

At dinner-time we were given a fair share of the food that Abel cooked. There was boiled fish, and a kind of spongy white pudding with currants, which he had been taught to make by a retired cook of the English Navy, and which he called Spotted Dick. It lay so heavily in our stomachs that I thought of the story of the wolf that was cut open in his sleep and filled up with stones. It had the same effect on us, of taking the fright out of us, so that all the long afternoon we could do nothing but lie there slackly in the sun. It was Louan himself who arranged that we should sleep comfortably in bunks that night. Michel and Abel did not want to allow it.

"They only make trouble," said Michel, glaring at us like an angry little sheep. "Let them sleep on the deck."

"No, no," said Louan. "It is I who am injured by them, and I say they must have beds."

Michel shrugged so high that his ears disappeared beneath his shoulders, but he said no more.

In the dawn of the morning, when we awoke, the long undulating line of the north coast of Brittany was just visible at the foot of the pale sky. By eight o'clock we were slipping quietly towards the mouth of a wide, smooth river. Ahead of us we could see the little town of Kerronan, built on both sides of the river with a bridge between. Below the bridge there was a stone quay with a great many fishing-boats. On either side as we came in, vast craggy granite rocks were scattered, lifting their huge heads out of the dropping tide like basking sea-dragons.

Now Big Dan himself was at the helm. I thought as I watched him that I would not care to try my hand at getting a ship of that size to harbour through those wicked waters. It was plain that he knew every inch of them, and that it was not for nothing he was the captain of the *Saint Ronan*. He was enjoying himself too, as we could see. He even forgot to glare when we came out on deck to watch the ship being moored to the quay. He cocked an eye at us, full of arrogant pride.

"It's not every man could do that," he said. "I've seen many a mug with his boat hanging on one of those rocks, like it would be hanging up to dry. You've got to learn to take your overightance—that's the whole secret, that and using your brains. It's a skilled job, of course. It takes skill and brain-power to do it right. And experience."

It was as well for us that he did not expect a reply, for we could never have supplied a civil one. He had already seen in our faces that we admired him as a navigator, and that was enough. He turned away with a great sweep, and began to shout noisy instructions in Breton to the men on the quay who were catching the ropes as they were thrown and tying them to bollards. We saw a boy run off in the direction of the town, evidently on an errand for Big Dan.

A great pile of boxes was waiting on the quay. Now several of the men took them aboard. The hatchway that led down to the tank was opened up, and everyone began to catch the lobsters and pack them into the boxes. They had canvas on loops of strong wire to catch them with. Tom and I stood on the deck and watched with interest, for we had never seen this done before. Then at my elbow I heard Big Dan snarl through clenched teeth:

"Idle, good-for-nothing loafers! Lazy young scoundrels! The youth of the country is gone to the dogs, to the dogs!"

So I pulled at Tom's jersey, and we went down and helped the men to fill the boxes. Big Dan snorted once or twice, but he could not bring himself to thank us.

Each time that we came out on deck, I looked up along the quay towards the town. A little bend of the street cut off the view, but above the shining slate roofs of the houses I could see the tall spires of a cathedral and a gold-handed clock on a tower. Sounds of loud talk and laughter came from there too, though there was hardly a soul to be seen except for the men who were working at our boat.

I asked Louan if something was going on up there in the town. He heaved a long sigh.

"It's the day of the market," he said. "The best day of the whole week. All my cousins will be in from the villages around." He stopped suddenly. "But it does not matter. In a few weeks I'll be here again. It does not matter, missing one market day."

He shuffled heavily away from me as if all belonging to him had died.

On one of these trips on deck, I saw that a horse and cart had arrived from the town. In charge of them was the same boy whom Big Dan had sent away earlier. Now we began to load the lobster-boxes on to the cart. They were to go to the railway station, Louan said, and then to Paris by train, seven hundred miles.

"Everything goes to Paris," he said disconsolately. "Everything."

And just then Big Dan came backing out of his cabin, carrying one end of the Viking's box. At the other end was little Michel, chattering:

"It's quite heavy. I think it must be full of gold. What's in it, Captain?"

"Feathers," snarled Big Dan, with such an ugly look that Michel fell into a terrified silence.

I kept out of sight lest Big Dan might see me watching him. All the time, while they carried the box down the gangway, and loaded it on to the back of the cart, and while the boy drove off up the quay towards the town, it seemed to me that I could hear the faint, cold, distant music of the Singing Cave.

Everything goes to Paris, Louan had said. For a single horrible moment it occurred to me that the Viking might go there too. I knew that if he were put on that train I would never lay eyes on him again. When I went to Galway, I was capable of getting lost between Eyre Square and the docks. If I were to follow the Viking to a city the size of Paris, my chances of finding my way out again, before old age would catch up with me, were small indeed. Then I remembered that the Viking was to be put into a cave. Though I was ignorant enough of the geography of France, still I knew that Brittany and not Paris is the place to look for caves.

Big Dan planted his feet wide apart on the quay and bellowed up to Louan and Tom and myself, who were hanging over the side of the *Saint Ronan*.

"Not a foot off that ship, d'ye hear? Not a foot! Louan! You keep a close eye on those young blackguards. Not a passport between them, I suppose. And not a red ha'penny. Proper knights of the road, they are!"

By this he meant that we were tramps or beggars. He stayed for a moment longer to enjoy the rage that he had aroused in us, and then he swung off up the quay towards the town. Without looking at us, Michel and Abel scuttled down the gangway and trotted after him. Within a few minutes, all three of them were out of sight.

"Ah, well," said Louan philosophically, "It is a pity that you can't see the market."

During the next hour, Tom and I strove continually to get away from Louan, so that we could plot our escape. But each time that we seemed to have succeeded, he would stroll suavely up to us and join in the conversation as if we were all the best of friends. He intended to carry out Big Dan's orders, it seemed, having become resigned to the necessity of it.

Then we saw a boy of about Tom's age running towards us from the direction of the town. He ran with his head down, elbows bent and feet pounding as if he were pursued by an angry crowd. Louan looked up too. His face turned a queer yellow colour. His mouth became hard and indrawn, like the mouth of a toothless old man.

"It is my son, Ronan," he said in a little, dead voice.

Ronan paused at the foot of the gangway and looked up at his father. Very slowly he began to come on board, talking as he came. We could not understand a single word of the conversation that followed, for it was all in Breton. But by their gestures, and the tone of the words, and by the changing expressions of their faces, we could guess very well at what they were saying. We were proved right when Louan turned at last to us and said softly:

"Our brave capitain has told everyone that I am here, but that he will not allow me to come ashore. To my own people he has said this—to my wife and my children, and to my cousins who are all in the square today for the market. He has laughed at me, and said that I am like a bad boy whom the teacher will not allow to go home with the other boys.

Look at my fine son, Ronan, how he is suffering!"

It was true indeed that Ronan was bitterly humiliated, and angry with his father too for allowing Big Dan to make him look foolish. Still he was watching Louan expectantly as if he hoped that he would yet prove himself a man. Louan saw that look, and all at once he seemed to swell up with determination. The colour came back into his face. He whirled around and seized Tom and me by an arm each.

"Come along! We'll all go to the market! And if Big Dan does not like that, then I can go back and work for the sardine fishers."

By this time, the turn at the top of the quay had become for me as mysteriously painful as the road in a picture on our kitchen wall at home. Now in the last few hours it had seemed to me just as unlikely that I would ever see the town of Kerronan as that I would penetrate into the world of that picture which had tantalized me since I was a baby. And turning the corner at last was doubly wonderful, because of the strangeness of the scene that was there laid out before us.

It was a great regularly shaped market square, which reminded me at first glance of our own market in Galway. There was a huge stone cathedral at one side, just like ours—but this, after all, was the only resemblance.

The first difference was that there was a long line of stalls running right around the square. Everything that one could possibly want to buy was laid out on these stalls. There were clothes, and bales of cloth, and toys, and fruits of all kinds, and vegetables, and small hardware, and tools. There were huge stalls of cakes, coloured so brightly that they seemed to shine like lamps in the sunlight, red and green and yellow. There were necklaces and earrings and brooches, more beautiful than any I have ever seen, even in Galway.

And if you could take your eyes off the stalls, the shops all around the square were at least as wonderful. Most of them had put tables outside, to display what they had for sale. There were several cafés, with round marble tables right out on the footpath, so that the customers could sit there and watch the fun, shaded from the sun by tall, striped umbrellas.

Louan hustled us past all these marvels, so that we had time only to say to each other: "Look! Look!"

Presently, at a tall, thin house directly facing the cathedral, we came to a stop.

It was the only house for yards around that was not a shop. At one side of it there was a wool-shop, with great hanks of coloured wool in piles on a table outside. At the other side was a cake-shop, which smelt as I hope heaven will.

Through the open door of the house we went straight into the kitchen, where Louan's wife was just taking a huge tray of freshly baked jam tarts out of the oven. She was short, and as round as a twenty-gallon pot. She wore a dark-coloured skirt which reached almost to the floor and a red embroidered blouse. On her head was a beautiful snow-white cap, made of lace and pleated linen.

For one moment after we came in, she held her tray high and stared with astonishment and then with delight. Very slowly and carefully she put the tray down on the table and came over to speak to Louan. Neither Tom nor I understood her words, of course, but as with her son, language hardly seemed necessary. Her face, her hands, her whole body expressed her pleasure in Louan's return, her feelings of hospitality towards us, her anger with the captain and her pride in her husband that he had not submitted to Big Dan.

Presently also it became clear that she intended to celebrate. She went to the door and called out several names like trumpet-calls, loud enough to be heard at the far side of the market-place. Then she stood poised on one foot, almost blocking the light that came through the doorway with her broad girth.

Within a few moments, children began to trot up to the door, like horses in their heavy wooden sabots. She stepped aside for a moment to let each of them into the kitchen. There were three little boys whose ages ranged perhaps from five to eight, and two girls who looked older. She peeked outside again, after they were all in, and then she came in herself and gave them instructions.

Louan sat comfortably by the stove now, pulling at his pipe as contentedly as if he had never left home. Though the heat was almost painful, we went to stand near him for the feeling of friendliness that he gave off with his pipe-smoke. The children watched us intently all the time that they were listening to their mother. It was like being watched by a row of intelligent, good-natured mice, but it made us uneasy, for all that.

"She's sending them out to collect all the cousins," said Louan with a sudden laugh. "She is a good wife. We'll all have jam tarts and cider. It's a very good thing to come home."

Now the three little boys darted outside again. Through the open door I could see how one went to the right, one to the left, and one crossed the square by climbing under the stalls, until he came to the cathedral steps. There I saw him talking to a woman who was selling lace from a basket, and busily making more while she waited for customers. I had noticed her because she was wearing an astonishing cap, of white lace, about a foot high and very narrow. She paused in her work when the little boy pulled at her sleeve, and leaned down to listen to him. Then, very quickly she folded up the lace that she was carrying on one arm for sale, and stuffed it into a basket at her feet, and followed him out of sight.

Meanwhile the two girls were helping their mother to spread a heavy white cloth on the table, and to lay glasses and plates enough for a regiment. They put the fresh tarts on to huge platters, and one of the girls went out to the shop next door for cream cakes. Then they rolled two stone jars of cider out of a corner and stood expectantly by the table, waiting for the party to begin.

Within twenty minutes, it seemed to us that we were as firmly imprisoned in that kitchen as we had ever been on the *Saint Ronan*. Between us and the door there was a wilderness of lace caps and embroidered shawls and chatter. The men, who made up half of the company, wore faded light-blue cotton trousers and dark-blue shirts and blue berets. They congregated around Louan, and shook his hand, and kissed him on both cheeks, a sight which filled us with amazement.

Soon everyone, including ourselves, was holding a glass of cider and a jam tart. The heat was such that if I had put out my hand I could almost have felt it. Faces were beginning to get red and damp. A fat man made a long speech to me in Breton, poking me earnestly in the chest all the time with a sausagey forefinger. When I made no reply he was not in the least put out. I think he took my silence for profound wisdom and discretion, for presently he put his fingers on his lips with a knowing air and moved off in the direction of the cider jars.

"If we don't get out of this soon," said Tom's voice in my ear, "we'll fall down in a weakness and they'll all trample on us."

He began to push his way towards the door, pounding at stout blue or embroidered backs until they moved aside and let us pass. The party had overflowed from the house right out on to the footpath. At the very edge of it we looked back and saw that more cream cakes were being handed into the steaming kitchen over the heads of the crowd.

To cool ourselves and to collect our scattered wits, we began to stroll gently around the market, pausing often to admire the things laid out for sale on the stalls. I wished I had some money to buy a pipe all carved with leaping horses, for my grandfather. There was a whitish wood in the bowl and a darker kind in the stem, and it had a beautiful little amber mouthpiece.

Then, while I was examining it under the watchful eye of the woman who owned the stall, Tom said quietly into my ear:

"Look there, by the cathedral. It's Big Dan."

10

On the Trail of Big Dan

t was Big Dan, all right.
He was talking to a
short, round-headed
man who was dressed in a black frock-coat
and a wide black hat, instead of the usual
shirt and beret. Apart from these he had an
air of importance, perhaps because he did not
smile. He listened to Big Dan with a slight
frown, as I have often noticed people do when
they wish to appear wise.

Then he took Big Dan's arm and began to
lead him down the side street that ran by the
cathedral.

I laid the pipe gently back on the stall. The
woman sighed with disappointment.

"We'll follow them, I suppose," I said
morosely, "though I don't see what good that
will do. If we get near enough to hear them,

same, we won't understand what they're saying. Oh, Tom, I'm afraid this has been a sorry journey. At home on the quay at Barrinish we could have done something. We could have got my grandfather down to help us, and Lord Folan and Patsy Ward. They would have made Big Dan open up the box. They would have been a match for Mr Allen. But now here we are in a strange country with no friends to help us. We've lost the box, and it looks to me like we'll never find it again."

While I spoke, we had begun to move towards the side street after Big Dan. I was so absorbed in my own woe that it was only now I noticed that there was a third member of our party. Louan was walking softly just behind us.

I stopped dead, with my head down like a depressed old cow at Galway Fair. Tom walked on a step or two, and then turned to look at me. Louan took the chance of moving in between us. He seized my arm and shook it, and spoke in short, jerky sentences:

"I saw you come out. I followed you. No one missed me, though the party is to celebrate my return. Where is your courage? Did you have no cider? There is a lot of courage in one of those jars of cider, very sure there is." He laughed and shook my arm again. "I have my courage back. I heard what you were saying. Never say you have no friends to help you."

"Friends," said Tom quickly. "That's what we need, sure enough. Who is that man with Big Dan? The decent-looking man with the hat?"

"That is our Mayor," Louan shrugged. "He is a good man but not very clever. In Kerronan we do not like our Mayors to be too clever."

"What is Big Dan doing with him?" Tom said. "That's what we'd like to know. And we want to know what he did with the big box he was minding so carefully in his cabin the whole journey over. That box has something in it that belongs by right to Barrinish. We want to know where it is now. That's why we came to Kerronan, not to lose track of the box."

"You didn't come to see the world at all?"

"Of course not," said Tom contemptuously. "We could see the world any time, and a lot better, from a hooker!"

Where we stood, it was as quiet as a country road, and dark where the shadow of the great cathedral cut a diagonal line across the cobbles. At the top of the street the sun poured down on the bright stalls, and the people moved and turned like brilliant butterflies. No one even glanced in our direction. This seemed very strange to me. In Connemara we are not so polite, or so indifferent.

Louan was looking from Tom to me, first with a kind of blank astonishment and then with sudden joy.

"Do you mean that our brave capitain is a voleur, an assassin, a dishonest man? Do you mean he has jiggery-pokery in his sleeve? Oh, I have waited a long time for this! I will tell you something. Listen! Often when we were on voyages, I smelt rats, but I could never pin them down—"

By this time, Tom and I were almost helpless with laughter. Tears ran down our faces, and we had to lean against the cathedral to prevent ourselves from breaking in two with the pain in our sides. Louan was not in the least offended. He stood there grinning, looking from one of us to the other in a friendly way, though he was clearly a little puzzled to know what had amused us so much. Tom said at last:

"Jiggery-pokery and rats up his sleeve is right. And there may be worse to come. When Big Dan walks with that little swing, he's usually up to something."

"Down there is the Town Hall," said Louan, pointing to the end of the street. "That is where they are gone, I am sure. Yes, because our Mayor always takes people to the Town Hall. It looks well."

It was a fine stone building, two stories high, and with great square windows shining like polished copper in the sun. As we went towards it we saw that part of the building was supported on arches of stone, under which the street ran, down to the bridge that we had seen from the river estuary.

"There is the Council Room," said Louan pointing to the three windows above the arches.

Then, while we watched, two heads moved across the glass. For one breathless moment we waited for them to come over to the window and look out, but they did not. Instead they came to rest opposite the middle window and began to nod earnestly to each other like courting pigeons. Louan whispered to us to be silent, and we slunk down the rest of the street like three oversized cats, until we were too close to the building to be seen from above. Louan pulled us into a tiny huddle by the shoulders and said into our ears in a soft hissing voice:

"They are sitting at the Council Room table, quite near the window. The window-frames are old. I am going to try to hear what they are saying."

Against the middle arch, under the middle window, there was a beautiful sculptured statue of a woman in a hooded cloak. Her shoulders were hunched. Her hands lay hopelessly in her lap. Every line of her spoke of despair and sorrow. On the base some words were written in French.

"It is the war memorial," said Louan, taking off his beret from respect and stuffing it into his hip pocket. He pointed to the inscription with his toe and read out: "'Never forget the children of Kerronan, dead for the fatherland.' She will not mind if I use her in a good cause. Pardon, Madame!"

And he stepped from her pedestal to her knee, from her knee to her shoulder and thence to her head. It was all done so respectfully that no one could have taken the least offence. Up there, he did not seek to steady himself by shifting his feet. Indeed he seemed to wish to cause her the least possible discomfort.

The top of his head came just under the

window-sill. He leaned against the wall, as if he hoped to hear through the stone. Watching him from below, it seemed to us that at first he heard nothing, for he cocked his head from side to side like a listening dog. Then he went very still. In agony we kept looking up the street towards the market, and down between the arches towards the bridge. If someone happened to look this way, we knew that they would be able to tell at once what Louan was doing. Standing there on his strange perch, he was quite unmistakably an eavesdropper.

Our relief was enormous when at last he climbed very quietly to the ground. Again he took our arms, and trotted us underneath the arches and down the hill towards the bridge. We kept to the footpath, past the Central Hotel, from which came an immense and sudden smell of dinner and a hungry clatter of knives and forks on plates, past an over-grown park that ran down to the river-bank, and past a long curving row of shuttered stone houses. Then we came to the bridge. The river was muddy here, and not very deep, so that no sea-going boat could come so far. Still the bridge was built with a swinging part in the middle, like the bridge at Béaladangan that can be opened to let the hookers through.

"Maybe in the time of the Vikings this was a good river for ships," said Louan, who had noticed how we looked from the bridge to the muddy river and back again. He laughed shortly. "Vikings! There is a buzzing in my head. I will tell you what I heard—no, walk along fast! There is no time to stop. I heard our brave, good capitan tell the Mayor that last night we anchored off the coast here below where I will show you. He said he went ashore into the singing cave that is there and found a Viking sitting in his boat, with a game of wolves beside him."

"But if that were true," I burst out, "the Viking would have been found long ago, when that cave opened first."

"Our capitan says that the back of the cave must have been closed off until the last storm. He says that everything could be washed away in the next storm. So he is going to bring the Mayor there now and show it to him. The Mayor has promised him money, a reward, because the Viking will go into the museum of Kerronan which up to now has only a few old shells and stones in it. The Mayor is very pleased, because many people will come to Kerronan now, to see the Viking and his wolves, and they will stay in the Central Hotel which belongs to his fat cousin from Tregastel, and they will buy souvenirs in the market and cakes and cider in the cafes and everyone will be happy and rich."

He had to stop then because he had used up all his breath. We were seething with rage by now so that it was a long time before we could put our story in order for Louan. Piece by piece we told it as we walked along. At last Louan said with a sigh:

"Of course I can see what Big Dan thinks of. After all, Mr Allen did say the Viking was to be put into a cave. So there is no harm in making a little extra profit."

This was the first time that he had called Big Dan by his right name. There was such a depth of wistful understanding in his voice that we had to turn our eyes away from him. For a second it occurred to each of us that he was still capable of going back and helping Big Dan to work out his plan. I could swear that he saw no moral reason why he should not. He had little respect for museums, as we could tell by the way he had spoken of the one at Kerronan. And he had no respect either for the Mayor of Kerronan who was to be led by the nose to this bare-faced hoax.

But then he remembered how Big Dan had disgraced him with his people and his anger flared up again. We fanned it as best as we could, and were pleased to hear him use some very strange words to describe his brave capitain. A toad, a pig, a dog he called him, savouring each word as if to test its suitability.

In this way we walked along briskly until we had left the town behind. We passed some fine stone cottages by the road-side, each with its field of various vegetables of enormous size. We were filled with envy especially at the sight of the potato fields, some of which were already being dug, although it was only April. Ours would not come into flower until June.

Presently we came to a narrow pathway on the left-hand side of the road.

"We will take this way," said Louan. "It will be quicker. And besides I must send a message to my son Ronan by one of the sardine-fishers. You said you told the circus man, Patsy, to make your grandfather come after you in the hooker."

"Yes," I said, "but the hooker could not be here so soon. Though she's a fine boat, she's not as fast as the *Saint Ronan*."

"You're forgetting how we were delayed at

Kinsale," said Tom. "She could be here in the next few hours, to my thinking."

"And I don't want her to come sailing in to Kerronan Quay," said Louan. "Your grandfather is an old man. No doubt he is excited or worried because you are gone. Perhaps he would ask the people where you are. He might even go to the police. We Bretons are not naturally a curious people, but when our curiosity is aroused we are formidable. We poke the nose into everything then—oh, we are disgusting, I swear to you. So I will get one of the fishers to tell Ronan to take out our little sailing dinghy and meet your grandfather and his hooker at sea."

"How will they understand each other?" I asked.

"You are making difficult," said Louan crossly. "Ronan will make him understand. He is a clever boy. He could make the stupidest person understand. He will tell your grandfather to sail the hooker around to the quay at Kermanach."

We made no more objections. Louan seemed to know what he was doing, and since we did not, it seemed good sense to leave the rest of the arrangements to him. He led us very purposefully along the little path, which ran without fences through the open fields. Cottages were scattered here and there with only a vein from the main path leading to the door of each. Some had patches of beans and potatoes beside them. We began to smell the sea again, and presently the cottages were festooned with fine trailing nets which looked like hair.

At a place where the patch took a sudden right-angled turn around the corner of a cottage, Louan stopped and looked in through the open doorway.

"This will do," he said to us, "if Yves is at home."

And he led us into the kitchen. A tall thin woman was standing by the stove, earnestly tasting a spoonful of soup from a huge black pot. Her face was like a peanut, long and yellow, though she was not old. Her pale tongue, when it darted out to lick her lips after the soup, was like a peanut's kernel. Still she seemed good-natured when she smiled at Louan, and at each of us in turn.

Yves was no farther away than the potato field, she said, and she went to fetch him in.

"She is his sister," Louan explained with a sigh. "It is a pity she is so yellow, for she is a cook of heaven." He threw his eyes upwards.

"Her soup, her stew! They would not give an angel indigestion. She would make a wonderful wife."

And he shook his head sadly.

When Yves came in we saw that he was thin and yellow too. We were given bowls of the soup, and fresh sardines fried in butter. It was a heavenly soup, as Louan had said, and though we were both aware of the danger that it might turn us yellow, we finished it to the last drop. Louan drank some too, while he talked, with a melancholy eye on the peanut lady.

From Yves's little exclamations of astonishment and approval, it was easy to see that he was willing to undertake the task of finding Ronan and sending him out to meet my grandfather. Better than this, he offered to come back at once when he would have delivered the message, and sit in his boat offshore near the cave after we would have taken the Viking away, and watch the arrival of Big Dan and the Mayor. They would never guess that he knew anything about the Viking. Even as he spoke, Yves let his long face take on that expression of sardonic boredom that fits these people so well, and shrugged with one shoulder. Louan laughed with delight, and translated the conversation for us so that we could enjoy it too.

Soon after that we continued on our way to the shore. There were fewer cottages now, because the land was hilly and wild, with a pale salty look on the grass that we knew well. When I looked away to the west I was surprised to see that evening was falling. All along the horizon were great piles of grey woolly clouds. I pointed them out to Tom, and said:

"If this were Ireland, that would mean there's a storm coming."

A moment later we felt the light wings of the wind flutter over us with a little sighing sound. Then we came in sight of a long, rocky shore.

There were granite rocks, glittering palely in the evening sunlight. They were scattered here and there over a stony beach, which narrowed at one end where tall cliffs overlooked the sea. Down there, Louan said, was the singing cave. The tide was so far out that it was no more than a long grey-blue line just below the horizon. Still he said that when it would come in it would cover the whole beach almost up to the grassy verge.

"Now, follow me!" he finished. "Like ducks

we will go, I in front and you behind me. We must be fast but careful. There is still a great deal to be done."

He led us down on to the beach by a tumbling sandy path. Then instead of crossing directly towards where we knew the cave to be, we kept to the top of the beach, walking unsteadily on the heavy rolling shingle. Presently we came to a place where the sand had been scooped out of the low cliff above us to make a little shelter. Here Louan stopped and turned towards us.

"Fish-boxes," he said. "Yves said I could have them. We will take one each."

Tom laughed and said:

"I never thought of boxes. Did you, Pat?"

"No," I said in astonishment. "I did not."

They were big boxes. We took one each. Carrying mine on my back like a snail, I wanted to run along the shore now that we were so near to success. But like a snail, or an old man, I had to take my time. Around and over and between the rocks we went, watching every step, until it seemed to me that I had never in all my life looked on anything except pale brown glittering rock. When Louan stopped at last I lifted my eyes and found with astonishment that we were standing before the tall narrow mouth of a cave in the rocky face of the cliff. Below us, the sea was moving closer in great rolling white-edged curves.

"Now we must hurry," said Louan, "before the sea is at the door."

And he walked cautiously into the cave.

11

We Find an Old Friend and Start for Home

shall never forget the excitement of those first minutes. It caught me, somewhere low in my vitals, so that I could hardly place my feet on the ground with the tingling that ran through them. This cave was bigger than our singing cave at home, and the dark brown rock, all broken in sharp angles, looked quite different from our smoothly-worn grey limestone. Instead of stone scattered with dry silver sand, the floor here was hard brown sand, packed tight by the pounding sea. All around us where we stood at the entrance the wind sang a high unearthly song through invisible apertures and crannies in the wall.

When we lit matches, and went in to the back of the cave, there was the Viking with a helmet on, leaning back against the remains of the prow of his boat. He looked even more tired than when I had seen him first. Big Dan had not been able to make him sit up so straight, I suppose. It occurred to me then that he would never sit up straight again. On the floor in front of his feet was laid the game of wolves. It was all like the kind of half-waking dream where you feel that you have done the same things, and have been in the same places before.

I sprang on the game at once. Not a piece was missing. I lifted a wolf out and stroked it, and called Tom away from the Viking to look at it. Louan came too, holding a match close so that the polished ivory glowed. It had been cut so cleverly that the little teeth shone whiter than the rest, and in the flickering light of the match it seemed that the round wicked eyes flashed red. Tom gave a long sigh.

"What kind of a man must Mr Allen be, that he would send a treasure like this away in the hands of that pirate Big Dan? If he kept it himself, same, and had it to hold in his hand every day, he should be the happiest man in the three kingdoms."

"He's a dry kind of a man," I said apologetically; "he doesn't feel things like other people."

"I'd as soon be dead," said Tom with contempt.

But I was thinking that once, long ago, Mr Allen must have been different. When he began to study first he must have been able to feel excitement and wonder in a simple, ordinary way. Now it seemed that he had lost the knack of it, so that he really deserved our pity. I started to say some of this to Tom, but Louan interrupted, shaking frenzied hands at us:

"You are like Frenchmen for searching out the philosophy, and reasons, and principles. We have no time. If the tide comes up on us, or Big Dan and the Mayor, there will be an end of all argument. Into the box, my friend!"

Under his direction, we packed the Viking, and his helmet, and his boat, and his game into our boxes. We hoisted them on our backs and started to make our slow way out of the cave. I thought of the many journeys that this Viking had made. It did not seem right to be disturbing him again so soon.

At the mouth of the cave, we held back while Louan peered around to see if it were safe to come out. In a moment he signalled to us, and we followed him cautiously out on to

the beach. This time he led us to the left of
the cave, instead of going back by the way
that we had come. He did not speak until we
had rounded the corner of the cliff that cut us
off from the main part of the beach. Here we
were quite near the sea. It was hurrying
every moment closer in long growling waves
which were blown up into little rearing jets of
spray by the rising wind. It was a lead-dark
sea edged with white.

Louan gave a little exclamation.

"Here comes Yves already."

We looked along the line of the coast towards Kerronan.

A sardine-boat with red sails was tacking
expertly towards us against the wind. We
watched her in silence for a moment. Then
Louan said:

"In the lee of the cliffs he will be able to
heave-to and look busy at something until Big
Dan comes along."

He turned his back on the sea and began to
climb up over the rocks towards the long
rising grassy slope above the shore. We panted
after him.

"Shouldn't we wait for a signal?" I said.
"How can we be sure that he has given the
message to Ronan, or that Ronan will be able

to go out in the dinghy and meet my grandfather?"

Even loaded as he was, Louan managed an
expressive shrug.

"It would be very nice, perhaps, to wait and
have a chat with Yves. But I do not want to
have a chat with my brave capitain on this
beach also, and that is what will happen if we
do not hurry. No, no. Yves is a good man. He
would not deceive us. And his coming now
with his boat means that he has already
spoken with Ronan."

Tom looked at me and gave a beautiful
imitation of Louan's shrug. There was no
more to be said after that. We struggled along
behind Louan without speaking, for we needed
all our breath for our labours. Since that day,
I have always been very civil to our donkey
when I take him carrying creels of seaweed
on the beach. My back aches with his and my
feet know the weariness of his little hooves so
well that I cannot bear callously to force him
on.

At the top of the beach, just before we
started up the easier slope above, Louan
allowed us to pause for a moment and stretch
tall and wide. We looked back and saw that
the sardine-boat was riding at anchor off-

shore, rocking on the roughening sea but comfortable enough. Three heads bobbed busily about in her. Yves had brought his crew, of course. We could see the whole of the beach from this point. There was still no sign of the Mayor and Big Dan.

"Good," said Louan. "Now we can go on."

Up the long slope he led us, over the rough grass, through furze and thorn bushes, through a wood of tall slender pines that swayed like the masts of ships, until we looked down on a little village of white houses, curving around the edge of a tiny bay. Louan said:

"That is Kermanach. Down there lives my Cousin Anna. But we cannot bring our boxes down until it is quite dark. I will go down now and tell her that she is going to have guests. It is a fine thing to have cousins everywhere."

And he trotted off down the hill, chuckling to himself, before we had time to ask him any more questions.

We sat down among the new green ferns, wrinkled like young butterflies' wings. The wind blew cold up here. An angry red light glared from among the heavy clouds just above the sea. Soon it would be dark. We knew that

Big Dan must have discovered his loss by now, and in spite of our own uneasiness, we thumped each other with delight at the idea of how he would squirm under the Mayor's questions. But presently we lost heart again, and as the dark climbed slowly over the hill we fell into a weary silence. Lights came on in the little village below us, so that the bay was outlined in a semicircle of yellow jewels. Through open doorways we saw people, no bigger than matchsticks, trotting busily in and out. Then one by one the doors were closed and we knew they were having supper. It was lonesome to think of all the families down there, sitting around tables of good Breton food while we sat cold and high like ancient hungry gods on the hillside.

It seemed an age before we heard Louan labouring up the hill again. When he was beside us, it occurred to me suddenly that he might not have returned at all. He echoed my thought himself, with a comfortable chuckle:

"Did you think I was not coming back? Did you think that perhaps I had just walked off to Kerronan by the field path, and left you sitting?"

"No, no," I said in embarrassment.

Tom was silent, so I knew that this had

We Find an Old Friend

occurred to him too. Fortunately Louan did not pursue the point. He sighed happily.

"My cousin Anna is a fine hospital woman. And her daughter Berthe is growing up just like her. They have begun to prepare supper for us. They said that we are welcome to stay in their house until the hooker comes from Ireland. So you see, we can sit in Anna's kitchen for hours if we like, perfectly happy eating our shellfish!"

He kissed his fingers and waved them in the air with pleasure at the idea of it. Tom said stonily:

"Is that the fine supper? Shellfish?"

"Yes, yes. Mountains of them! Barrels of them!"

"The blessings of God on us," said Tom, rising to his feet and hoisting his box on his back.

All the way down the hill he did not speak. I was glad that we had to go in single file. Louan trotted on in front, thinking happily of shellfish, and he did not notice that the same thought had silenced us.

Presently we joined a little path which soon in its turn joined a sandy road, and then we were in the village. Just to see the lighted windows made us feel warm and comfortable again. The wind was from the land, so that we were sheltered from it by the houses. Louan's cousin lived in the nearest house to the quay, he said over his shoulder as he still bustled along ahead of us.

It was small, like all the houses in Kermanach. It was built end-on to the road, so that whether the wind blew from the sea or from the land it did not blow in the door. I thought this a very clever and far-sighted arrangement. A stone's throw away was the quay. We peered into the darkness down there, in hopes that the hooker might already have arrived. It had not, but away out to sea there was a ship's lantern tossing on a mast. It was still no more than a dull point of light in the thick gloom, but my heart rose at the sight of it.

"I'd swear that's our boat," I said into Tom's ear.

He stopped in his tracks and called softly:

"Louan! There she is! It's not worth while going into the house. We'd be better to wait at the quay for the hooker and board her at once."

But we were not to be let off so easily. Louan stood gazing at the lantern for a moment and then said:

"She's beating against a head wind. It will take her more than half an hour to reach the quay. And anyway we could not allow you to start your long journey home with empty stomachs. We are a hospitable people, just like the Irish. It is a matter of honour with us to give our guests a meal, especially guests from a foreign country."

So we had to go into Anna's house, and leave our boxes against the kitchen wall, and sit down to plates piled high with shy shell-fish. We had cider to wash them down with, and great long thin loaves, like walking-sticks, with butter. Anna and Berthe were cheerful and jolly, and they smiled with satisfaction as they watched us eat.

Even a meal so little to our taste restored our courage. Soon we were impatient to go outside again and see how much closer in the hooker had come, but Louan would not allow it.

"You would do well to keep out of sight," he said. "We must not have a curious crowd on the quay watching you embark."

"Then you are not coming with us?"

He puffed his lips in and out speculatively.

"I would like to come. Yes, I would like to come. But I must have work. And I cannot work on the *Saint Ronan* any longer. I was told to stay on her and I did not. Big Dan will know at once that I helped you to move the Viking out of the singing cave. Now I must go back to the sardine-fishing."

"Is that not such a good thing?" Tom asked.

"Sardines are smaller than lobsters," said Louan impatiently. After a pause he went on: "Some time perhaps I will come to Barrinish. I would like to know the end of this story, for I will tell you it is the strangest thing that has ever happened to me."

"Things like this don't happen to us every day of the week either," said Tom dryly. After a moment he added: "And we would like to return your hospitality by giving you a fine dinner of potatoes and sour milk."

Louan bowed politely but the idea did not seem to make him happy.

Presently he sent Berthe out to see how the hooker was faring. When she opened the door, we could hear the wind whistle past. It was not a storm, but a fine hearty cheerful wind that would blow you to America if you were not careful.

"The sooner the hooker comes in the better," I said, "for that wind will take us home as fast as if we were in a train."

"If it doesn't change," said Tom.

"It won't change before tomorrow," said Louan, with certainty.

We sat silently then, while he and Anna chatted in their own language which sounded so strangely like ours. We became drowsy from the heat and the food. The soft murmur of their voices was like music or the twittering of birds to us, because we could not understand their words.

Then suddenly Berthe was back in the kitchen again, in a whirl of petticoats and shawls and smoke puffing down the chimney. She was a fine tall girl, a few years older than ourselves, and with a great air of knowing what she was about. Her hair was light brown, smooth and shining, piled in huge plaits on top of her head. She was bubbling over with excited laughter. She threw her hands in the air and skipped around the kitchen with little chuckles of delight as she spoke to Louan and her mother.

"Ha!" said Louan after a minute or two of this. "Yves is at the quay. Yes, yes, the hooker is there too. But wait! I must tell you what Yves saw at the singing cave—Big Dan and the Mayor and three of our most important citizens from Kerronan. So slow, so slow they had to climb over the rocks. The Mayor is not young. The most important citizens are fat. They eat well because they are rich. They puffed and blowed. They tore their most important clothes. Oh, it was a pity to see, Yves said. They came to the cave all red and shiny. Big Dan was the only one who was cool. He is accustomed to taking exercise. Yves sat and mended his nets quietly while they went inside. When they came out again it was Big Dan who was red and shiny. He had to run." Louan rolled about in his chair with laughter at the thought of it. "Yes, he had to run, and the Mayor and the three fattest and most important citizens of Kerronan ran after him. This time they did not mind climbing over the rocks. They hardly saw them, they were in such a hurry to catch Big Dan."

"And did they catch him?"

"No," said Louan regretfully. "He got away. They did their best, but he got away. Ah well, we cannot have everything in this world, I suppose. It was something that he had to run."

"I'm glad they didn't catch him," I said, "so long as we have the Viking."

"I would like if they had caught him," said Louan venomously. "He made me look foolish before my own people and that is a terrible thing to do to a man of my years. And besides, now he is free he can follow you home to Ireland. He looked like murder, Yves said." He shrugged. "It is no wonder. He can never come to Kerronan again. That will make him angry. Kerronan is a nice little port, and the lobsters are plentiful there, and the train takes them direct to Paris."

By this time, of course, we had shouldered our boxes and were ready to go. Louan gave our thanks to Anna and Berthe for their kindness and told us that they wished we would come and visit them again. Then we were outside in the shrieking wind, staggering under our loads down to the quay.

Our hooker lay alongside the quay with her nose pointing out to sea again. Beyond it was Yves's sardine-boat, rising and falling on the uneasy water. Against the dim light on the pierhead I saw my grandfather standing on the quay, waiting for us. He grasped my hand and shook it, as soon as I had laid down my box. Not a word of reproach did he say about my going off without him.

"Both safe and sound?" was all he asked.

"All three of us," said I, tapping the Viking's box which Louan had laid beside mine.

Within five minutes we were aboard, and the boxes were stored in the lee of the little fore-deck so that they would not get splashed. It was going to be a wet passage. We could see the white-capped waves blown backwards by the wind outside the little harbour.

" 'Tis a good wind for us," said my grandfather.

Yves had come ashore now and we could see that Ronan was with him as well as the three members of his crew. I liked the look of Ronan, and would have been glad to know him better. They all stood on the quay above us waiting to help us cast off.

"Louan!" I called out at the last moment. "You come to Barrinish with Yves, in the sardine-boat, soon. And bring Ronan with you!"

"Yes, bring Ronan with you," said my grandfather. "He's the cleverest lad I've met in a long time. He explained where I'd find you, without using a tongue or a language."

"We'll come, we'll come," said Louan. "God speed ye, and a safe journey!"

These two fine wishes he had learned in Ireland. It made me lonesome to hear them. On a dark stormy night, I thought, it is a good thing to be able to go home to your own bed, as Louan and Ronan were about to do, instead of tossing off into that cold, black wilderness that lay outside the harbour wall.

In a moment we had hauled up our main-sail. Louan and Yves threw our mooring ropes on board. The hooker left the quay at once, without even the smallest push from a foot. She filled with the fine wind and in a moment she was streaking off out of the harbour before it. Dimly in the light on the pierhead we saw Louan and Yves and Ronan wave to us, before they were hidden by the wall.

Once outside the harbour, the boat settled down to the long, comfortable roll that we knew so well. At this part of the coast the rocks were not so plentiful as at Kerronan, or we could never have expected to make the open sea. One or other of those wicked granite teeth would have been sure to snap at us as we passed. We were silent while we trimmed our sails and set our course, and lit a second lantern. Then we all sat together in the stern of the boat while my grandfather rummaged for his pipe and got it going. After a puff or two he said:

"The wind will smoke it for me, I'm thinking. Well, Patsy gave me your message. A nice message that was—to take out the hooker at my time of life and sail off alone to Kerronan."

"We didn't want that," I protested. "I thought Lord Folan would have come with you, or even Patsy himself."

"Patsy has to mind his circus. And he has no love for the sea, though he's an islandman born," said my grandfather. "And Lord couldn't come on account of the currach races. He had to get his currach ready—she was needing a patch by the bows. And there was the chance that we wouldn't be back for the start of the big race. That would be a terrible thing."

"Are the races so soon?" Tom asked in astonishment. "I have lost count of the days since we left home."

"Saturday morning, day after tomorrow," said the old man. "With this wind we'll just be in time for them. Mind you, if I'd asked Lord he'd have dropped the races and come. But I didn't ask him, of course, for it would be a cruel thing for the whole of Barrinish if he wasn't there to make a fight of it with Rooster."

Now I realized the size of the task that we had laid upon my grandfather. Though he had the name of being a powerful man in a boat, still it was a great long journey for a man of his age to undertake all alone. He could have asked my father to come with him, but it would have taken time to go over to Brosna and call him. Besides it would be a matter of honour for him not to ask my father for help in looking after me.

It was only then, to the sound of the creaking timbers and singing sails, that we told the old man of Mr Allen's treachery. He was silent for a long time. At last he sighed and tapped out his pipe on the ballast at his feet, leaning over so that we could not see his face.

"Ah, well," he said. "I always knew that Mr Allen was a strange man. Living alone without wife or child has driven him in on himself, I suppose. It could happen a man like that, that he'd end by thinking books are more important than people. And then how could he know what friendship is?"

This from a man who usually thought well of everyone was very bitter. It showed us plainly how deeply he was disappointed in Mr Allen for deceiving him. Since I had lived with my grandfather, I had learned the wickedness of breaking up old friendships. Seeing him discover Mr Allen's weakness gave me no satisfaction, no feeling of superiority. It only made me want to weep for the smallness of human nature, and to wish that all fine honest men like my grandfather could live apart in some place where they would never meet anyone less clean than themselves.

We slept by turns that night in the smoky little cabin. It was sweet sleep, in spite of the suffocating discomfort, for the smoking turf was Irish and the fish whose ancient stench mingled with it had been caught in Irish waters.

When I climbed out of the cabin in the morning, the sea was emerald-green streaked with white. For a moment only, our ship seemed very small as she climbed and plunged over the towering waves. But a following wind is always sweet, and a glance reassured me that the hooker was making her way home as confidently as a horse to the stable. The thought ran into my mind that if we were shipwrecked the Viking and his possessions would surely be lost. It did not occur to me then, I swear to you, that we would have a hard time of it ourselves trying to swim home to Ireland in such mountainous seas.

Tom was below in the stern, hauling in mackerel one after the other on a line.

"These will make a better breakfast than shellfish," he said to me. "I don't know why

they're abroad in such weather, but their
misfortune is our luck."

We roasted them over the hot turf in the
brazier and ate them with soda-bread. My
grandfather had not forgotten to bring plenty
of bread, of course. He snorted when he heard
how we had set off empty for a foreign land.

"I wouldn't like to travel far with the pair
of ye," he said. "Always when you start on a
journey, you must at least bring two days'
food. If you eat for two days you can fast for
the third and no great harm done."

The journey to Brittany had seemed endless
though we had had bunks to sleep in and had
eaten well. With all its discomforts, the journey
home was over in a flash. We tended the
sails, and fished, and chatted, and slept, all
in such an unhurried way that we would not
have minded spending a month on that hooker.
The wind dropped a little on the evening of
the first day, but it was still strong enough to
drive us along firmly. All of the second day it
stayed the same, so that in the evening Tom
said:

"If it's no worse than this tomorrow, they'll
be able to have the currach races, all right."

On the third morning the sea was no longer
green. Instead it was a deep indigo, touched

here and there with white. Just above it, as far as we could see, the clouds made a huge city of dark-blue towers and castles. Quite early, flocks of seagulls gathered screaming around us. Away off in the distance, a tall grey shadow was Black Head, at the mouth of Galway Bay. The Aran Islands stretched lazily at its feet.

Then, as Tom and I peered ahead for the first glimpse of Barrinish, my grandfather said quietly:

"Look astern, boys. It's the *Saint Ronan*, or I'm Finn MacCool."

12

At the Sports

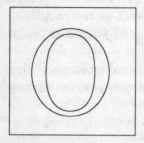ne glance told us that
he was right. The *Saint
Ronan* was so different
from any other boat that visited Galway Bay
that even at such a distance we could identify
her. She was plunging and tossing as un-
comfortably as ourselves, but like ourselves
she had the advantage of the following wind,
and with her engines she was making far
better speed. Tom and I looked at each other.

"I'd like to be on dry land at least, when
next I meet Big Dan," he said.

My grandfather asked sharply:

"Are things as bad as that?"

"They are and worse. Louan said he'd be
ready to do murder, after the big nobs of
Kerronan would be finished with him. Of
course we could make for Black Head. 'Twould

be nearer than Barrinish."

But I would not agree to this.

"We have good friends in Barrinish, and a thousand places to hide the Viking. Half the battle is won if you're on your own ground."

" 'Tis true for you, of course." Tom measured the distance between ourselves and the *Saint Ronan* with his eye. "And maybe we'll just make it."

"Of course we'll make it," said my grandfather heartily, but I could see the gleam in his eye that only came when he was excited. Also by the way he kept turning his head to look back at the *Saint Ronan*, I knew he had his doubts. Even in the few minutes since we had seen her first, she had shortened the gap between us.

During the next hour we watched her slowly crawling closer.

"If she has any lobsters in her tank now," said Tom, "they'll be standing on their heads with the speed of her."

My grandfather tried to divert us with stories of the preparations for the sports. He said that there were only two entries for the old men's sack race, Johnny Gill and Michael Ban, an old neighbour of my own from Brosna. Johnny was the favourite. His trainers had promised to give him a practice gallop on the very morning of the race, so that he would be well limbered up. The sports were to start at twelve o'clock with the currach race, which was the most important event. After that would come the jumping and the pony races and the tug-o'-war, as well as all sorts of other things, and at night there would be the circus to finish off with. A familiar shiver of excitement ran up and down my back before I had time to remember that if Big Dan had his way I was not likely to have much time in which to enjoy all these delights.

When we came inside the curve of Norseman's Bay, the sports field was already black with people. It was a long, smooth, beautiful field right by the quay. A stranger would have said it was far too good a field to be wasted on sports, but we knew that it was no use planting crops in it because at the spring tides or when there was a storm it was often flooded. The strange thing was that it belonged to Johnny Gill, though it was more than a mile from his house. In summer he grazed his terrible old white cow there. She had the meanest milk in the four islands. On many a summer evening, I and my friends had to jump the ditch and run off when we saw

Johnny begin to climb painfully over the stile out of the field, after he had milked his cow. If we had met him he would have offered us a drink, warm from the can. We would have had to accept from politeness, but we were prepared to go to great lengths to avoid it.

As we came in closer we could see the currachs lined up on the shore. A little crowd standing near we knew would be the owners and their friends and relations. Great black clouds hung low over the island. Above the noise of the wind and waves, the strange wild sound of the Singing Cave filled the air. I could see that very soon we would learn to measure the strength of the wind on Barrinish by the volume of that sound. The line of houses above the quay gleamed white where a long beam of cold sunlight fell slantwise across the hill. At the top of the quay, the grey cone of Patsy Ward's circus-tent flapped in and out frantically.

" 'Tis almost like a winter's day," said Tom. "I'm thinking they won't be able to launch the currachs after all."

"They've gone out on worse days," said my grandfather. "They won't be put off by a little blow like this."

Soon we saw that this was true. One by

one the currachs were being carried down to
the water's edge. Then each one had its oars
put aboard and was lifted high on the
shoulders of three men. At a signal, all three
dashed waist deep into the water through the
first breaking wave, set the currach on the
heaving sea and then flung themselves into
her. It was all done in one great splendid
rush of movement. Though I had seen this
manoeuvre many, many times, it never failed
to fill me with a bursting excitement. I threw
back my head and let out a great bellowing
cheer for the heroic men of Barrinish.

From a little way behind me, came an
answering bellow of rage. It was Big Dan,
standing in the bows of the *Saint Ronan*. His
fists were alternately grasping and clawing
the air. His knees and elbows were bending
in and out as if they worked on springs. His
teeth shone white with fury, like the waves
that tumbled on the rocks of the reef, or like
the teeth of the little snarling ivory wolves
that lay in the bottom of our boat. Tom and I
looked at each other in terror. Tom said, in a
voice gone cold and quiet with fear:

"He's going to ram us, Pat, as sure as
there's a tail in a cat. If he does the old man
will be drowned."

I hardly heard him. At that moment I had seen an astonishing thing. All the people on the shore and the men in the currachs had begun to wave in answer to Big Dan. At that distance they could not properly see nor feel his rage as we could, and they thought that his shouts were encouraging cheers. Big Dan's arms dropped to his sides. Now Lord Folan's currach was flying towards us. The waves made such hills and hollows that each time the three men bent to the oars, they disappeared as completely from view as if the sea had swallowed them up. As they came closer, Lord began to shout over his shoulder to Big Dan. My grandfather laughed softly, and slapped his knee with his open hand.

"I know what Lord wants," he said and he chuckled again. "We're in luck today, boys, and no mistake. Lord is going to have the *Saint Ronan* for a mark in the currach races!"

It was quite true. Big Dan had to switch off his engines and drop anchor right there and then. As we sailed impudently under his bows on our way in to the quay, we could heard Lord in his currach shouting to explain that it was only for an hour. Lord was very polite, always.

"I'm heartily thankful to you, Dan," he

said. "We used to have a buoy here, grand
and handy for the currachs to go round it on
the day of the sports, but it got washed away
on the night of the big wind in January and
we're a bit slow putting it back. Of course
we'll have it for next year, never fear. It's
only the once I'm asking you to do this for us,
knowing you have plenty of time to spare, for
there won't be a lobster sold in these parts
before Monday. Thanks and thanks, again,
Dan, and may God spare you your health."

"Half an hour would do us nicely," I said.
"We'll have our boxes safe where a bigger
Dan than that couldn't find them, in half an
hour."

We whistled and sang all the way in to the
quay. We got a beautiful berth by the steps.

"You'd think 'twas left specially for us,"
said Tom skipping ashore with the first rope.

Two minutes later we were shouldering
our boxes up the quay. Our plan was to take
them straight to the Clooney Cave. Big Dan,
being a foreigner from the Achill Island, did
not even know of this cave's existence. We
knew that if he came nosing too close to it in
the next few days, everyone in Barrinish would
combine to divert him in another direction, by
fair means or foul.

At the top of the quay we paused, just to throw one last triumphant careless glance towards the *Saint Ronan*. She was riding solidly at anchor, as she always did, while the waves crashed uselessly against her sides like kittens playing around a sleepy mother cat. And where there should have been two little figures and a big one hanging resignedly over the rail, there was nothing. My eye darted at once to Lord's currach, now more than halfway back to the shore. Crouched in the stern, almost buried in the waves, was Big Dan. Two tiny huddled lumps in front of him I knew must be Michel and Abel.

I stopped dead, and pointed with my free hand. Big Dan was gazing fixedly in our direction.

"From where he is, he'd see us starting on the road to Clooney," said my grandfather, after a pause. "And 'twould be easy for the three of them to follow us. There won't be a soul out Clooney way today. Everyone is at the sports. We'll never hold our own against the three of them."

"We must change our plan, then," said Tom impatiently. "Come along—down to the sports field!"

I hung back.

"But that's where Big Dan is going. We'll walk right into his arms."

"And he'll have to bid us the time of day, as civil as a lady," said Tom firmly. "He won't dare to attack us when we're surrounded by our own people."

"Tom is right," said the old man. He was looking anxiously at the currach. "That's a big load that Lord has. I'm thinking he'll be a happy man when he lands his three passengers safe."

Only that the currach was overloaded, we should never have reached the sports field before it came ashore. The other currachs that were to take part in the race were bobbing about just outside the breakers. They all closed in to advise Lord how best to land his passengers. We could see Rooster's red head stretching up on his long neck as he clamoured for attention. Then came warning shouts and shrieks of laughter as all the currachs came in too close and were in danger of being washed ashore. When they paddled back swiftly to the safer waters outside, we saw that Lord's currach was grounded on the sand, and he was helping his three passengers painfully to climb ashore. By the time this had happened, we had had time to run the short distance from the quay to the sports field and to dispose of our boxes.

It was Tom who decided what to do with them. At the edge of the field a platform had been built to a height of perhaps two feet above the ground. It was to be used for the singers and bagpipers and melodeon players later in the day. Old Luke Duffy had insisted that there should also be a competition for story-tellers, and already when we came along he was sitting up there on a kitchen chair, thumping with his stick as if he were at a fireside and giving out a long story in Irish about the rescue of a princess by the King of Ireland's son. No one was listening to him, of course, except the teacher from Lettermullen, a polite young man called Hynes who was said to have a great interest in folk-lore.

Silently I obeyed Tom's signals, I crept after him, into the space between the platform and the ground, and there we laid our boxes in a row. My grandfather gave his to me, for at the last moment he was not able to stoop low enough. It was the first sign of his age that he had shown in the whole business, beyond his mild complaint at having to sail alone to Kerronan.

Arranging the boxes was slow, for we were

afraid to make the slightest noise. Right beside us, Mr Hynes's feet were resting one on top of the other in a tired way. The sight of them made me uneasy, almost as if they could see. Just above our heads, Luke Duffy thumped with his stick and droned out:

"Then the King of Ireland's son drew his pistol and shot the Giant of the Three Heads stone dead. But his troubles were not over yet. They were not, faith, and it's not a bit of good thinking they were..."

We heard Mr Hynes sigh, and his feet shifted so that the top one was now resting underneath. We crawled silently out from under the platform and rolled about on the grass, in the hope that anyone who happened to see us would think we were only playing about like pups. In the middle of this I looked up and saw the Tailor limping past. He was wearing his Sunday suit of good blue serge and a new grey tweed cap whose peak was still stiffly straight across his forehead. This gave him an unfriendly appearance, and I also thought that it narrowed his view, for he gave no sign of seeing my wave of greeting.

In a moment we stood up, and moved casually about the field walking one at either side of my grandfather. Hoarse-voiced tinkers had stalls of sweets and oranges at the edges of the field. There was a game of roulette and a stall for shove-ha'penny. In front of a tall stand, a young man in a yellow waistcoat bellowed without ceasing a long piece of patter about his game of chance, always ending with the same words:

"The smallest child has as good a chance as the man with the watch and chain! Come in your bare feet and go home in a motor-car!"

A trick-o'-the-loop man had laid his coiled rope on top of a tall box and was gazing impatiently in the direction of the sea, where everyone was waiting for the currach race to begin.

"Come on, boys," he said hopefully to us as we passed. "Try your luck. Your chance is as good as mine."

"I'll tell you what," said my grandfather genially to the trickie. "Give me charge of the rope and let you do the betting for a change."

The trickie made no reply. He was a little, dirty man, not dirty in lumps like a country man but sort of grey all over, as if he had never washed in his life. He looked fixedly at my grandfather, and then he rolled up his rope quickly and dropped it into his pocket. As we walked away, we saw him pick up his box and move it to the far end of the field.

"A city man," said my grandfather with contempt. "They're easily frightened."

Then we saw Big Dan. He was moving through the crowd without greeting a soul. His eyes were narrowed. Their whites glittered evilly as he darted glances from side to side under his eyebrows. The people took one look at him and then slipped out of his way without a word, recognizing, I suppose, that for him they were as dead as gravestones. We saw him pause a moment like a pointing dog when his eye lit on Sarah Conneeley, Mr Allen's housekeeper. She was his sister, as I have said before, but I often forgot this because their names were different.

Sarah was talking rather distantly with some of the wives of the seven Seáns. Three of the Seáns were manning a currach from Le Clé in the race that was about to start. Big Dan marched roughly up to the group, seized Sarah by the arm and almost dragged her away. She had to run a step or two, or she would have fallen. He led her to a clear space a little away from the crowd. We circled them from all sides, and we could see Big Dan thumping the air with both fists while Sarah listened in her stony way. When she narrowed her eyes, now for the first time I saw how like her brother she was in spite of being so much thinner and smaller.

We watched while Big Dan finished his speech and whirled around, and marched off towards the stile. He sprang out over it, with no more than a hand on the wall to help him, and strode thunderously up the road. As he approached Bartley Connor's public-house he slackened a little and wiped his mouth in an anticipatory sort of way, with the back of his hand. A moment later he vanished inside.

"Look at that!" said my grandfather. "Good riddance of bad rubbish. Though mind you I could do with a pint of the black cow's milk myself." He sighed and went on: "It often surprises me, how a cross man is twice as strong as a quiet one. Did you see the way he jumped that wall?"

"Look at Sarah," said Tom quietly. "She has found Mr Allen already."

They were standing very still, so that anyone watching them would think that they were discussing nothing more exciting than the weather. Sarah was looking demurely down at her feet, but I noticed that her head was on one side as it always was when she was making mischief. I think she imagined that it made her look innocent.

"Keep an eye out for Patsy Ward," said my grandfather. "After dark he'll shift those boxes for us, and none better than himself to do a job like that."

Everywhere we looked there was one of Patsy's children, but Patsy himself was not to be seen. We saw Michel and Abel buying big biscuits at one of the stalls. They ate them at once and washed them down with quick nips from a flat bottle that Michel had in his hip pocket.

In a few minutes, Sarah walked slowly back to the group of women with which she had been before. Mr Allen began to move about the field, smiling at everyone and stopping now and then for a moment or two to talk, as if he were quite content. Presently the tailor joined him, and walked with him, leaning heavily on his stick.

Now a shout from the beach sent everyone running down to find out what was happening there. The women from Le Clé swept Sarah along with them, and Rooster's sister, the Snipe. She always became very much excited at the races, and now her face was all twisted up as if she were going to cry.

Before we had time to follow them, Johnny

Gill came trotting up to us with an empty sack flung across his shoulders.

"Ha, boys! 'Tis a good thing ye're home in time for the most important thing. I thought I was going to have a fight for it," he chuckled, "but you can put your money on me quite safely, oh yes, quite safely. I'll tell you something, Michael Ban is too old! And he had to walk all the ways from Brosna at this hour of his life. He'll be tired, tired."

"You're away with it so, Johnny," said my grandfather solemnly.

Johnny chuckled again.

"And I have good supporters. There's nothing to give a man heart like good supporters. Are you supporting me?"

"We are of course, Johnny," we said.

"Maybe you're not," said Johnny to me. "After all, Michael Ban is a Brosna man like yourself."

"I'm a Barrinish man by adoption," I said. "I'm supporting you all right, Johnny."

"Ah, that's good. Mr Allen said the same. Did you see the fine sack he gave me?"

" 'Tis a fine sack indeed," I said.

"Oh, 'tis all that," Johnny chuckled. "And he's a good friend of mine."

Just then there came another wild shout of

delight from the shore. Johnny whirled around, and gazed towards the sea for a moment. Then he gave a little jump with both feet, very funny to see.

"Stop! Stop!" he called out, on a high wailing note like a seagull. " 'Tis the sack race first! We must have the sack race first or Michael Ban will be rested. There's time enough for the currach races afterwards."

He ran stumblingly down the field towards the shore. We ran after him, of course, for we wanted to see the start of the race. Johnny bored a way with his fists through the crowd. Tom and I followed him, but my grandfather had to be more polite, being older.

Johnny was dancing about with rage in the shallow water at the sea's edge when we caught up with him.

" 'Tis the sack race first," he was wailing. "And if ye won't have the sack race first, ye can be going out of my field."

Lord said soothingly:

"Sure, if we do that we can't have the sack race at all."

Johnny stopped, bewildered. Then after a moment he said:

" 'Tis true for you, Lordeen. You have the brains, for certain sure. I'll go back there now where it's quiet, and rest myself, and mind my fine sack."

And he turned and pushed his way back through the crowd again, as heartily as he had done in the other direction a few minutes before. We stayed right where we were. The people gave way to Johnny good-humouredly enough though one or two advised him to excuse himself for his rudeness.

The four currachs were lined up waiting for the signal to start. There was Lord's, and Rooster's, and the one from Le Clé, and a strange boat from Lettermullen manned by three fine men that I had not seen before. The presence of these had excited the Barrinish people; they did not want to see either of their champions beaten, but they hoped that the winners would have to put up a good fight. The harder the fight the greater would be their glory.

And now at last we had found Patsy. He was the starter of the race, and though we stood beside him for half an hour, we could not tell him a word of our trouble, surrounded as he was on all sides by our neighbours. He was standing on a low rock just clear of the spray. He had an ancient brass blunderbuss which I had often seen before. It was used in all of Patsy's plays where there was need for any kind of gun, from a cannon on the field of battle to a pistol for shooting a wicked baron with.

Now Patsy let off the blunderbuss with a tremendous roar that sent everyone near staggering backwards. When we had recovered, the four currachs were ten yards away, rolling on the dark waves, the three sets of oars going up and down sharply as the men alternately lay back on the thwarts and bent their heads down between their toes. Soon the boats were tossed wide apart by the waves and battered by the tearing wind so that they seemed to crouch low for shelter into the very sea which was so hungry to swallow them. As they moved farther out we saw them only by snatches when they rose to the top of the waves. If one of them had gone down, it might not have been missed for minutes afterwards.

During the agony of the next ten minutes, the people were tensely silent in face of the awful strength of that mountainous sea. Over all the land, the wailing of the Singing Cave was like the lonesome cry of the banshee, which is only heard when someone is going to die. Standing there gazing out at the little black specks now rounding the anchored lob-ster-boat, all at once I experienced a feeling of guilt, as if I had invented the Singing Cave, which I knew was filling all my neighbours' hearts with such doleful thoughts.

Then, as the currachs turned homewards, the people began to come to life again. The oars were shooting up and down as smartly as ever. Sure enough, Lord's currach and Rooster's were out in front. It was easy to see Rooster's wild red hair blown high by the wind. Lord was wearing his broad black hat with a tape under his chin to hold it on. The Lettermullen currach was next. Its three men had grey knitted caps. And last of all came the men of Le Clé, floundering a little be-cause their currach was not built for racing.

At my elbow Corny Lynch suddenly bellowed:

"Come on, Lordeen!"

My ear-drums quivered. Corny turned to me and said, confidentially:

"There's ten pounds of my good butter gone to greasing that currach's keel. Shout for Lordeen, Pat! Shout for Lordeen!"

So I opened my lungs and bellowed:

"Come on, Lordeen!"

A little distance away the Snipe shrieked:

"Rooster! Rooster! Rooster!"

Then she burst into tears and fell into the arms of her friends. All of Rooster's supporters had taken up the cry, however, and now his name was chanted rhythmically until it must have knocked holes in the floor of heaven.

We redoubled our yells too. We knew that the men could hear us, for the oars had suddenly begun to strike even faster. Tom and I joined hands in a frenzy of excitement and shouted Lord's name, and the names of the other two until our eyes popped and our throats were sore. Now that the currachs were coming nearer, I thought that my soul would fly out of my body to meet them and lift Lord's currach bodily ashore. With a last spurt it drew away from Rooster's. When it was a yard out from the shore, we all dashed into the water and dragged it the rest of the way. Our clothes were coated with a sad mixture of butter and tar and seawater, but we did not care. We ran with Lord up the beach on to the grass, and rolled about, and kicked our legs in the air, and stood on our hands until we had let out the feelings that were like to burst us. Then we lay there on our backs, looking up at the blackening sky.

Suddenly we heard a thin shout from the direction of the road. We sat up. The tailor was there, waving his stick and calling out something that we could not hear. Then a feeling of alarm rippled through the people standing around us.

"It's Lord's cattle," said a man beside me. "Tailor says they're running wild, up on the cliff."

13

On the Cliff-top

 was watching Lord when the news reached him. He was stretching his tired arms wide and laughing in his usual slow, good-humoured way. Now his arms dropped by his sides, and a look of anguish fell like a sudden shadow on his face.

"My cattle?" was all he said.

And he began to run with great, long, loose strides towards the stile. Rooster looked up from the middle of his crowd of friends who were offering consolation, mostly by saying that Lord had cheated in some way which they could not name. A moment later he had swept them aside and was running after Lord across the field. I saw them reach the stile together and stop for no more than a second. Then Lord clapped Rooster on the shoulder once, lightly. They skipped over the stile one after another and started up the road.

"I'm thinking we'll all be wanted," said Mattie Connor. "Come on, men, everyone that has a leg under him. 'Tis no easy job surrounding a herd of cattle that's gone wild."

"And they're in powerful condition," said Corny Lynch. "Lord always has the finest cattle in the islands."

"Fine they are," said Mattie, "and as strong as Protestants, every one of them."

As the men moved like a huge black tidal wave towards the road, it was plain that the sports were over for a while. Seeing this, the women began to leave the field too, most of them intending to follow the men and take their part in the drama on the cliff-top, and some to slip in home and have a cup of tea and a gossip. Of course all the children were already galloping around and around the men to be sure of missing nothing. My grandfather came hurrying over to us.

"We'll have to go too," he said in a low voice. "Keep your eyes open. How lucky this had to happen now."

"But the Viking?" I said.

"A live cow is worth a sight more than a dead Viking," said my grandfather sharply.

"And all the cows in Ireland aren't the equal of a good neighbour. The Viking will have to take his chance. I've had one word with Patsy. He'll keep an eye on the boxes, and take them out from under the platform when he gets a chance."

This was our only comfort as we hurried after the crowd. I paused to look back, and saw Luke Duffy still sitting on the platform, thumping away with his stick. Mr Hynes, not being a farmer, would not have been expected to help in the rescue of the cattle, but I saw him look up hopefully like a sheepdog that has been left in a field to mind sheep, and that sees his owner approaching at last to release him. With a sudden movement, he seemed to make up his mind. He darted away from the platform at a staggering run, and in a moment he was lost in the crowd. Luke half stood up. He shouted and waved his stick after Mr Hynes, who now for all his patient listening was to be bitterly blamed for deserting his post at last. Then the old man began to climb painfully down off the platform, using his chair as a step.

I could not wait any longer without attracting attention. Already Luke was hobbling towards me. It did not take much brain-power to tell me that if I stayed there it was I who would have to hear the end of the story about the King of Ireland's son, and while Luke had an audience, that story would have no end.

By the time I reached the wall, the people were streaming up the quay road. Tom was waiting for me, but my grandfather had gone ahead with Mattie and Corny Lynch. My grandfather had a reputation as a strategist where cattle were concerned, and I could guess how the three of them would now be plotting their tactics as carefully as if it were the battlefield of Fontenoy.

"If we go with them," said Tom, "we'll have to pass Bartley Connor's door."

I stopped with my foot on the stile, imagining Big Dan standing at the door of the public house with a frothing pint glass of porter in his hand, watching the people hurrying past. I could almost hear his howl of rage when he would see us among them, and feel his hot breath on the back of my neck, like a hero fleeing from a giant in one of Luke's stories.

"We'd better go by the shore," I said. " 'Tis quicker, too, and we might be more useful there."

At the back of the quay, a steep beach

curved around to the end of the cliffs. Down by the sea it was sandy, but the top was a mass of round stones, worn quite smooth by the heavy winter seas. Above that was thin grass and rotting seaweed, softer to our bare feet than the murderous rolling stones. Here, away from the houses, the seagulls swooped and cried all around us, with that high, cold, light call that they give before a storm. There is always a special sense of hurry in this cry, whether from fear or joy I have never been able to fathom. Now it made us fly over the desolate ground, so that in a few minutes we were at the end of the beach, with the sandy face of the cliff a shadowy grey before us.

We left the shore and began to climb the grassy slope. Soon I glanced back to see the roof of our house, and a tiny triangle of whitewashed wall just showing above the sheltering shoulder of the hill. I had not seen it since that far-off evening when Tom and I had walked over the mountain road and had spied on Mr Allen through the window of Cashel House.

As we moved higher up, presently we could see the white road wriggling down past all the houses until it reached the quay. Here and there, one or two stragglers were hurrying after the crowd which had by now disappeared out of sight under the hill.

We kept well back from the cliff's edge, because the wind was charging across the hill like an unbroken horse. We knew that if we were careless it would sweep us along with it and over the top. The sky was lower up here, and inky black. I felt a few heavy drops of rain on my face, mixed with a mist of salty spray. The beating of the sea seemed to shake the very ground under our feet. And all around us, drowning even the roar of the waves and the intermittent shrieks of the wind, was the long, high call of the Singing Cave.

We were almost at the top of the hill when Tom clutched my arm and pulled me to the ground.

"Listen! The cattle!"

The wind snatched the words from his mouth so that I hardly heard them. Side by side, we laid our ears to the ground. There it was, a rhythmic thundering, that quivered through the thin grassy sod. We leaped to our feet again, and then stopped dead. A yard or two away, just on the crest of the hill, the wild black face of Lord's young bull was glaring down at us. Many and many a time, I had admired the great wide sweep of his magnificent horns, but never before had they seemed as powerful as now, when we waited from moment to moment for them to toss us to Kingdom Come.

For a full minute he stared, while we stood motionless and stared back at him. Then he turned slowly and plunged off down the hill by the way that he had come. In one leap we were at the top of the hill and gazing downwards. And there below us we saw an extraordinary scene.

The whole herd of little black cows were wheeling and circling together on the sloping side of the hill. Frantically they plunged and stumbled and tossed their poor bewildered heads. They galloped stiff-legged and whirled their nervous tails and let out terrified moos that should have melted a heart of stone.

But they did not melt the hearts of the two people that were now, as we could plainly see, deliberately trying to drive them to their deaths over the cliff. One was a thin woman in a red petticoat which flew out all around her like a sail. It was a moment or two before I recognized that this was Sarah Conneeley, for I had never seen her look so excited before. The other was Mr Allen. There was no mistaking him. Though he looked so frail and harmless, even at this distance, he was well able to trot up and down, waving his stick and poking at any cow that tried to break away from the herd. It was such a wicked sight that for the first time in ten years, I burst into tears of rage.

I started to run down the hill, but Tom gripped my shoulder and shouted into my ear:

"Look at the bull! There's why he had no time for us."

He had placed himself between the herd and the cliff's edge, and was charging up and down there, expertly turning back any cow that came too close to the danger. Sometimes he succeeded in turning the whole herd back, so that they galloped a little way down the hill. When this happened, Sarah and Mr Allen headed them off and sent them back up again. Tom laughed.

"They'll never drive them over as long as that bull is there," he said. "We needn't lift a finger. In less than ten minutes the men will be up from below, and they'll catch Mr Allen with his hand in the till. We needn't stir."

But he was wrong. At first I could hardly believe my eyes. There was Sarah, running up by the side of the herd, fumbling at her waistband as she came. She had dropped her shawl far away down the hill, where it lay a little whitish splash on the green. Now suddenly she stopped. Her red petticoat dropped about her ankles. She stepped quickly out of it, and began to run straight towards the bull. She was able to go much faster now that she had only her grey cotton petticoat to hamper her. Still we watched her in amazement, not knowing what she was going to do.

Right up to the bull she ran, quite fearless in her excitement. With a great whirling sweep, she lifted the red petticoat high and flung it over his head, and began to tie it firmly around his horns with the strings.

Immediately he wavered, and let out a bellow which should have burst Sarah's eardrums, since it sounded so loudly to us.

And now at last it was time for us to run, faster than we had ever done in our lives, for there was Mr Allen deliberately setting about driving the whole herd towards the cliff again.

Without their protector they were as helpless as a pen full of hens when the fox is at the door. They ran hither and thither. They ducked their heads and mooed most pitifully. Sarah left the bull, as soon as she was sure that he was firmly tied up in the petticoat, and ran back behind the herd. Tom and I made for the bull, Tom to try and disentangle him from the petticoat, and I to carry on with his work of keeping the cows from the cliff's edge until he would be free to do it himself.

You may be sure that in the next few minutes I would have been glad to have had a pair of horns. Painfully now I remembered how Johnny Gill had said that horns are useful things. Again and again the cows came at me, snorting and stamping, each time narrowing the gap between me and the cliff. With every rush forward, my terror increased. I shouted and waved my arms, but neither Sarah nor Mr Allen took any notice. Sarah was in such a state of exaltation that she seemed not to care whether or not we were witnesses of her villainy. As for Mr Allen, I think now that he had intended to say, if he were accused later, that he was trying to keep the cattle away from the cliff's edge.

Looking back on this terrible scene, what I chiefly remember is the noise—the wind's unceasing roar, the sea's crash and rumble, the wavering, piercing song of the cave and the urgent hollow thud of the cattle's hooves. This last was redoubled by the fact that they

were drumming on the very roof of the cave,
as we were soon to discover.

Out of the corner of my eye I saw Tom still
struggling with the bull. He had his knife out
now, and he was trying to cut away the heavy
flannel without jabbing the blade into the
bull's head. Sarah was hallooing and flapping
her skinny arms. With her grey petticoat and
her grey hair blowing wildly around her, she
looked for all the world like a scald crow. I
shouted to her and waved my arms too. For
answer she gave a little skip, with pure bad
temper, that almost made me laugh in spite
of my predicament. Then Mr Allen sent the
cattle rushing forward again so that I was
forced out on the spur of the rock from which
I had rescued our bullock, on the night when
I first heard the Singing Cave.

The cattle retreated, stumbling. Where they
had been, a wide section of the cliff's edge
cracked off, and pitched outwards, turning
slowly, until it disappeared from view. So
would I fall, I thought, and turn slowly just
like that, with the next onrush.

In a fog of despair I lifted my eyes. And
there, running up the long slope of the hill
were all the people of Barrinish. The men
were in front. From above they looked flat-

tened, like scurrying black-beetles. The children were little specks at either side, and a short distance behind came the women, looking like a flock of mixed hens and turkeys in their brown and speckled shawls.

I waved both arms above my head. I shouted until my voice went dumb. I sprang up and down so that I should be seen above the black backs of the cattle. And then Mr Allen turned his head and looked back.

Immediately, he stood still. The stampeding herd of cattle plunged past him on all sides. Now Tim had at last freed the bull. He was shaking his wide horns from side to side as if he still felt the confining flannel around them. Weakly Mr Allen lifted his stick as the last cow thundered past him.

And then came the strangest thing of all, so strange that I had to sit down right there on the spur of rock and gasp painfully for breath, and hold my shivering body with cold, cold hands to keep it still.

Quite slowly, the earth under Mr Allen's feet sank away from him. There before my eyes I saw him slide through into the very ground, without a cry, still holding his stick high. The grass was scarred and broken so that the sandy earth showed. A round black hole was all that marked the place where he had been.

And in that moment, the song of the cave died away.

14

Back to the Singing Cave

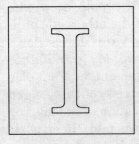t was Tom who hauled me in from the cliff's edge, and rubbed my face and hands, and made me sit up and look at the herd of cattle away down the hill out of danger. The bull had followed them at a little distance, and he had an air of being in charge of them again.

"Oh, Tom," I said, "did you see what happened to Mr Allen? Did you see it?"

"I saw it, all right," said Tom grimly. " 'Tis a judgment on him for his wickedness. Down into the Singing Cave he must be gone." He laughed shortly. "It must have been the trampling of the cattle that broke in the roof."

I was astonished at the simplicity of this explanation, and I think even a little disappointed. It had seemed so just that the earth should have opened up at that moment and swallowed Mr Allen in the midst of his sins. Then, as I began to recover my senses, of course I was able to pity him.

I got up on my shaking legs. Arm and arm we skirted the deadly little hole at a safe distance. Once we were at the other side of it, we began to run. Twenty yards lower down we met the first of the crowd. My grandfather was with Lord and Rooster out in front. He looked warm from the exercise, but it seemed that there had been no question of his lagging behind. In a few words we told them what had happened, and warned them not to go any higher.

"Right enough, I was full sure I had seen Mr Allen," said Lord. "We'll go around in the currach at once. There's a chance we'll get him out safe. You'll come, Rooster?"

"To be sure." Rooster took me by the arm and pointed to where Sarah had picked up her tattered red petticoat from where it had fallen, and was struggling into it. "In the name of all that's wonderful, what is she doing here?"

"She was helping Mr Allen to drive Lord's cattle over the cliff," I said.

"God bless my soul!" said Lord. He gazed at

Sarah for a full half-minute, as if he had never seen her properly before. Then he gave a shout of laughter and said, almost in admiration: "I never thought she had it in her."

Without wasting any more words, we left her to her undignified occupation, and turned to go down the hill. My grandfather had not spoken a word. I was almost afraid to look at his face, which had gone as cold and hard as rock at the news of Mr Allen's fate. Now when Lord saw how the old man was coming with us, he said softly:

"Will you look after the cattle for me, Mick? They have had a fright. 'Twill be a big job to catch them—"

"I'm coming with you in the currach, Lord," said my grandfather harshly.

Lord paused for a moment. Then he said:

"A man of seventy-two has no business out in a currach in a storm like this. 'Tisn't known if we'll ever get home."

"If we don't, then I'll be the one that will be least missed. I'll let you know in good time when I feel seventy-two. Mr Allen has been my friend for forty years. It would be a poor story if I wouldn't go to his help now when he has need of me."

In the end it was Tom who stayed behind.

To bring even four in the currach was dangerous enough, Lord said, but they would need three at the oars and one to attend to Mr Allen if it was worth while bringing him home. He glanced quickly at my grandfather as he said this, but the old man seemed not to have taken offence on behalf of Mr Allen.

The rest of the crowd surrounded Tom and began to demand explanations of what had happened. As we hurried down the long hill, I could hear their hoots of excitement. I wondered how much of the story Tom would tell them. They would not be pleased at hearing that we had found the Viking and had not told a soul about it, I knew. A good neighbour would expect to be admitted at once to such a secret. Still I hoped that the people would forget this grievance in the excitement of the things that were happening now. Only once I looked back and saw that all the women had surrounded Sarah and were doing a kind of derisive war-dance around her with their shawls spread out like wings. It served Sarah right, I thought, and I hoped it would occur to them to chase her all the way home to Le Clé.

After that I tried not to think of anything but the task before us. Huge drops of rain pecked at us, as hard as hailstones, borne on the heavy wind. All around us the sky was blue-black with cloud, except for one narrow streak of white, like a pencil-stroke, above the sea. The shut houses looked bleak and desolate as we hurried past. No comfortable smoke fluttered from their chimneys, and even the cluster of brown and white hens around each door had gone silent, having lost hope, I suppose, of ever being cherished again.

For me the tailor's house had always had a secret, closed look. Now I wondered if this were because he had no hens, nor even a cat around the place to give it life when he was not at home. And he had no half-door, but only a tall, blank one, that could not look friendly even when it stood open. I had noticed that he was not among the crowd on the hilltop, and I wondered if he were perhaps sitting inside at this very moment, hiding himself because he could not move as fast as the other men. More than once I had seen the look of pain that crossed his face when the men carelessly joked about the fine life of idleness that he led compared with theirs. And yet it was he who had given the alarm about Lord's cattle.

All at once, the truth struck me like a

blow, so that I almost tripped over my own feet as I ran. Until that moment it had not occurred to me that the driving of the cattle had been part of a well-laid plan. Since I had discovered that Mr Allen was a liar and a cheat, I suppose I had come to believe that he was a confirmed villain who would suddenly decide, for no reason at all, to drive a decent man's cattle over a cliff. Tomorrow perhaps he would steal a poor widow's goose, and laugh fiendishly as it crackled in his oven, or as he crushed its bones.

Now in a flash I saw that this was childish nonsense. The tailor had passed by with a cold unfriendly look, just after we had hidden the Viking under the platform. Later he had walked about with Mr Allen. And it was he who had come to empty the sports field by shouting that Lord's cattle were on the cliff. Now, far from sitting miserably within his house brooding about his infirmity, he was probably helping Big Dan to discover and remove the three boxes for the possession of which we had worked so hard. All this was perfectly clear. The only thing that puzzled me was why he should do all these services for Mr Allen.

The last part of the road back seemed from

that moment to have stretched like a piece of elastic. As slowly as a funeral, I thought, we trotted along. On the quay road, one or two doors stood open and elderly female voices cackled over pots of tea inside. The door of Bartley Connor's public house was open too, and I glanced inside to see if Big Dan were still honouring it with his custom. It was too dark in there, however. All I could see was the yellow face of the big wall clock, permanently stopped at five minutes before closing time.

Lord's currach was still on the shore below the sports field, but we did not go through the field to reach it. Instead we went down by the pier, and crossed the little stream by its rickety stepping-stones, and so came to the strand from which the race had started. I could not suggest to my grandfather that we try to see if the Viking was still in his hiding-place under the platform, for I knew that he would make the same reply that he had done before.

None of us dared look at the sea. The air was full of its savage growl. After each terrible wave had crashed to pieces on the sand, the backwash crawled hurrying after it like a cobra. Yet I remember that I was not very much afraid. How could I be, with my grandfather and Lord and Rooster to look after me? With those three, I would have set out for America in a wash-tub.

And Lord's currach was no wash-tub. Every line of her had been planned for speed and safety on just such a sea as this. We all took a hand in launching her, by the same method as I had watched with delight only a few hours ago. Holding her high on our shoulders, we waited until an extra big wave had come and gone. This we followed, running into the water over the crumbling sand, watching the huge wave cruising off out to sea like a man-eating whale on the lookout for a tasty bite. It was succeeded by a few smaller waves, as the whale is followed by a shoal of pilot-fish. We dropped the currach, which bucked and reared like a young horse, until our weight steadied it a little. In a moment the three men had the narrow oars in position. With the first stroke of them, the sea seemed to become calmer, as if it had recognised our right to ride on its back.

I crouched in the stern, drenched to the skin as the others were. Nearest to me, in the easiest place, was my grandfather. Behind him, Lord and Rooster sat relaxed and powerful, lifting and plunging their oars so easily that they seemed not to be using all of their great strength. It was wonderful to have them rowing in the same boat. In all my life I never remembered seeing this before.

"The three of you would make a fine team for the currach races in Galway," I called out suddenly.

"Ay," said my grandfather. "I'd be the brains and those two lads behind me could be the brawn."

But then his face went hard again, so that I knew his thoughts were not with us at all, but buried with his friend in the Singing Cave.

Lord, being in the bows, was in charge of the boat. He had no choice but to hug the shore. But if we came in too close, we might be thrown on to the rocks, and the thin canvas holed, and none of us would be seen again until the storm would be over. I was mighty glad that it was not I who had to decide how far in or out we should go.

As we passed the *Saint Ronan*, we saw that she was rising and falling now on her anchor chain, and swinging with the heavy tide. I wondered whether Michel and Abel had returned to her, or whether they had joined Big

Dan up in Bartley Connor's.

Outside the shelter of the quay wall, the full force of the wind struck us for the first time. With every wave, the currach rose up on her stern, before dropping again at the bows with a crash. The first time that this happened, I lay down on the floor as flat as a cat, and from that moment on I did not raise my head. Still I had no difficulty in seeing what was happening. If I did not look at the sea, the sea looked in at me, tall, curling, white waves with sagging jowls and slavering teeth, and shrieks like fifty devils whose tails are being stepped on. And I thought, how are we going to get an injured old man home to the quay under these conditions? The prospect of his weight added to ours in the currach was terrifying.

With such cheerful thoughts I entertained myself as we travelled along. Presently, at a signal from Lord, all oars except his own were shipped. I knew that we must be near the entrance to the cave. There was such confusion around us now that I could hardly spare a thought for what we might find inside. In front of me when I lifted my eyes, I could see the waves climbing the grey face of the cliff, almost to the summit. Clouds of spray blew up and over the top. I covered my face with my hands, as we seemed to make straight for that murderous wall, and then, quite suddenly, we were inside the cave and it was calm.

That was a blissful moment, before we leaped ashore, and moored the currach, and faced the broken stone grid that led into the back of the cave.

My grandfather was first through the grid. We followed him in a flash, and then stood in astonishment at the change that had come about within the cave. A gaping hole in the roof, like a long chimney, let in the daylight. The humming sound that had been all around us when we were here before, was now gone. Instead the wind swept in through the mouth of the cave and out by the open shaft, with a noise like thunder. Our feet on the sandy floor rang as clearly as if it had been a road, instead of in the curious dead way that I had noticed on my first visit.

Right under the hole in the roof there was a cone-shaped heap of mixed earth and sand. And spread out on the top of it, looking like a bundle of old clothes that had been thrown away by a tramp, was Mr Allen.

While we watched him, he stirred.

"He's alive," said Lord quietly. "Thank God

for that."

"He fell soft, I think," said Rooster. "There's no stones, only sand and earth."

We climbed the heap and stood in a ring around him. I thought he looked as if he were asleep, with his proud mouth shut and his limbs relaxed. But when my grandfather put out his hand at last and shook his shoulder gently, he did not open his eyes.

Lord knelt down and lifted his arms and legs one by one, and stroked them gently. When he moved his head a little, Mr Allen unconsciously wagged it impatiently from side to side. Lord stood up, saying:

"Ne'er a bone broken. 'Tis the like of him that have the luck. Straighten him out, there, Rooster, and we'll get him into the currach somehow."

Suppose he wakes up in terror when we're at sea, thought I. Suppose he leaps up in the boat, and sets it rocking, and it fills and sinks. The currach will be overloaded in any case, even if he remains asleep. It's a long, long way back to the quay. Mr Allen was old, not worth bringing home, as Lord had said. But because of him, three good men and a promising boy were to go to their deaths. All the time while I was helping the men to lift him and carry him to the cave mouth, I almost wept in sympathy for the people of Barrinish who would so soon be mourning our loss. Then, at the grid I turned and looked back, and saw a rope dangling down the shaft.

I almost dropped my share of Mr Allen.

"Look! A rope!" I exclaimed. "That will be Tom, using the good brains that God gave him."

They looked and with one accord we laid our burden down. We went back to stand on the mound of earth, looking upwards at the tiny circle of grey that was the sky. Then, cautiously, a head half-filled the circle, and Tom's voice called out hollowly:

"Hoy!"

"Hora!" Lord bellowed back. "You're only in the nick of time."

"Is he safe?"

"The like of him never comes to no harm," said Lord again. "And if you have that rope well secured, we'll send him up to you in two shakes."

"The tug-o'-war team is holding the rope," said Tom. " 'Tis the tug-o'-war rope."

"It ought to be strong enough, then," said Rooster. "If it was going to hold the men of

Brosna against the men of Barrinish, it can surely hold a little grasshopper like Mr Allen."

Though they spoke of him thus contemptuously, still they constructed a sling-seat from the end of the rope most carefully. They tested the knots many times before they laid Mr Allen in the loop. Then at last Lord called out to Tom, and the men hauled on the rope.

We stood underneath, looking upwards, ready to catch Mr Allen if the rope should break. Tom leaned over the shaft and held the rope steady, to prevent it from turning. From time to time we heard him call out advice to the men behind him. There was a terrible minute when Mr Allen had reached the top of the shaft, and Tom had to lift him bodily up through the hold. He could not have help, as we could guess, because of the danger of the extra weight of the helpers breaking down more of the cliff-top.

Just as the soles of Mr Allen's boots disappeared over the top, my grandfather turned quickly and said to me:

"We can tell Tom to let down the rope again. You can go up the same way. 'Twill be better for you than the currach."

"Is it go up that shaft, like a bag of oats going into the mill?" I exclaimed. "I'd rather swim home."

He did not press me. I was glad of this, for I did not want to explain how the sight of Mr Allen being hauled up that narrow shaft had revived in me all the horror I had felt at seeing him sink into the earth.

Now Tom was calling down to us again:

"All safe here. Anyone else coming up?"

"No thanks," Lord shouted. "We'll go home by the water, like Brian O'Linn. Carry Mr Allen carefully. You can bring him down to my place and put him in the settle bed by the fire where he'll be warm. 'Tis important to keep him warm."

"We'll do that," said Tom.

As we left the cave I saw Rooster's eye on Lord in astonishment. I knew that the same thought was in his mind as was in my own, that you would search all Connacht and its islands before you would find another man as charitable as Lord Folan.

We disposed ourselves in the currach in the same way as before, and glad I was that I could give my valuable self my full attention, instead of dividing it with Mr Allen. Still the knowledge that he was safe made the journey back to the quay seem easier.

The moment that the currach's nose ap-

peared outside the cave, the wind tried to nip
it off. Lord had his crew ready. The oars
struck powerfully all together and then we
were out among the hills and hollows beyond
the reach of the breakers. Crouched on the
bottom of the boat, I watched the waves of
dark cloud in the sky, seeming to reflect the
wicked dark waves all around us. The seagulls
that were following us in a shrieking crowd
dropped to the water's surface from time to
time and stared, as if they thought that we
would soon be as naked as themselves.

As we came nearer to the quay, I heard a
new sound above the creaking of the rowlocks,
and the roar of the storm, and the seagulls'
cries. I lifted my head and learned in one
glance what it was.

The *Saint Ronan* was under way. It was
the steady beat of her engines that I had
heard. Her black smoke was scattered over
all the sky, almost before it had had time to
appear from her funnel. She was plunging
and tossing so painfully that we in the currach
seemed almost comfortable, riding snugly on
the water like a seagull with folded wings.

I did not move, nor cry out. So great was
my rage and disappointment that I think I
went into a kind of trance. Even when I saw

my grandfather looking at me anxiously, I could not change my expression of misery, nor explain to him that now it was not fear for my skin that had overwhelmed me.

The rest of the journey seemed to pass quickly. Far too soon for my taste, we were in the shelter of the quay, and the desperate look had left the men's faces. I knew that I should be grateful to God and our patron saints for bringing us home safe, but all I could think of was the great helmeted warrior that I had lost again, and his game of polished ivory wolves.

Facing the shore as I was, it was I who saw Patsy first. He was running up and down the strand, pointing out to sea, stopping now and then to give a little jump of impatience, and shouting to us, something that was carried away on the wind. As we came in closer I could see several of his children behind him. The people who had been on the cliff-top were beginning to stream down the quay road.

Patsy never got his feet wet, if he could help it. He skipped in and out with the waves, and watched us haul the currach clear of them. Then he was over at my ear, shaking my shoulder as if to awaken me, and saying:

"Your boxes. I did all I could to hold them.

On my solemn oath, I did. But they're gone off out to sea. Alas and alas forever!"

And he gave a long wail like a dog. I said wearily:

"You did what you could, Patsy. 'Twas three to one. I saw the *Saint Ronan* going off, and we out at sea. I could guess what happened."

"No, no!" Again he shook me impatiently. "They're not on the *Saint Ronan*. That's what I'm trying to tell you."

He turned me bodily around so that I was facing the sea, and pointed with a shaking finger. Then he bawled out suddenly:

"Do you see that little black thing tossing around out there?"

I looked, and saw it.

"That's the currach of the men of Le Clé. And your three boxes are in it." Suddenly he was calm. "Listen, and I'll tell you how it was. Big Dan came down here from Bartley Connor's house, 'while ago. He had Michel and Abel with him. They made for them boxes, man, like demons. Myself and the Missis and all the goslings tried to stop them, but sure, we're small, and 'twas like sparrows trying to fight swans. They launched the currach of the men of Le Clé, and brought it around to the far steps of the quay, and they loaded the boxes into it. Big

Dan got very brave when that much was done. He stood up there on the quay, as bold as a robber's horse, and he shoved his two thumbs into his belt, and he told me he made out that what was in them boxes was very valuable, there was so much fighting to get them. So he was going to take them in to Galway and get a higher price for them there.

"But with that, I gave a sign to the goslings and they all made a drive together. 'Tis a good thing to be small, times. In between their legs and up on their backs they went, three to each man. Myself and the Missis got the towrope of the currach and we brought it out to the point on the quay. We got up on the high wall above— 'tis a good long rope—and we hauled out the currach until it got into the current. And between the current and the tide going out, didn't it float off out to sea. For said I to myself, if Pat don't have that Viking, Big Dan won't have him either. The big fellow ran around to the strand then, and they took Rooster's currach and they all rowed out to the *Saint Ronan*. They got aboard and turned her, as if they were going to go after the currach, but when they saw all the people coming down from the cliff, they made off towards Black Head. Now tell me honestly, did I do right?"

15

The End of the Story

f course you did right, Patsy," I said, still gazing hopelessly out to sea at the slow, black line that was all that stood between my Viking and destruction.

My grandfather agreed heartily. They had all three heard Patsy's story, but Lord and Rooster were now looking at each other in bewilderment. As we walked quickly up to the quay, we told them how I had found the Viking in the Singing Cave, and how Mr Allen had betrayed our confidence by getting Big Dan to steal it. Rooster's eyes sparkled. For a man who liked news, here was news indeed.

"How did ye keep that secret?" he said several times, in admiration. "How in the world did ye keep it secret?"

Lord, of course, was full of pity for Mr Allen.

"You'd have to have pity for a man as sour as that," he said. "Look where it has led him!"

"Pat," said my grandfather, in a low voice to me, "if we go out at once in the hooker, we might catch up with the Viking yet."

At once, the whole world changed. In a single bound, I came alive again. There was our hooker moored by the quay where we had left her. I boarded her in a flash and looked up at the astonished faces of our neighbours who were now surging all around us. I saw my grandfather speak to Lord and Rooster. Then to my delight, all three of them were coming down the steps on each other's heels. My grandfather climbed stiffly aboard. I began to haul up sail. Rooster had the boathook ready to shove off. Then, suddenly, Tom pushed his way to the front of the crowd and called out:

"Hold! I'm coming too!"

And a moment later he was on board. I saw his father, up on the quay, open his mouth and take a step forward. But he did not call him back, and a moment later we were out in the middle of the little harbour.

The tall black sail filled with the heavy

wind so that she heeled over at once. A shout of excitement went up from all the people, and they began to run towards the end of the quay. We could see some of them climbing the upper wall, from which they would better be able to watch us as we went out to sea.

Every timber in the hooker creaked and complained under the storm, but she fled over the waves like a bolting horse. After the currach, she felt as safe as an ocean liner. I climbed all over her, tinkering with the sails, and the ballast, and anything else that took my attention, until at last my grandfather said impatiently:

"For pity's sake will you sit down and leave the sailing of the boat to them that know how to do it!"

It was on the tip of my tongue to answer that without my Viking there would have been no need to go to sea at all. But when I saw that the old man was in a far worse state of excitement than myself, I went to sit with Tom. I lost no time in telling him Patsy's story.

"I wish I had seen that fight," said Tom. "Isn't it queer how Patsy is twice the man that Mr Allen is, though he's only half the size?"

" 'Tis the size of the soul that counts," said I. "How was Mr Allen when you left him?"

"Lying back in Lord's settle by the fire, wide awake. But there's not a word out of him. You'd think something queer is after happening to him."

"He fell forty feet into the Singing Cave," I said. "That must have given him something to think about."

"That's it, I suppose," said Tom seriously.

He said that Mr Allen had asked whose house he was in, and since he had been told, he had not spoken a single word. Lord's mother was in charge of him. She had the same cure for all ills, and that was poiteen and milk. She drank this mixture herself every night of her life, and at eighty-five she was as sound a woman as Lord's wife Bridget at half that age.

"Whether or which," said Tom. "Mr Allen is where he can do no more harm for a while."

Up on the quay, it had been possible to see the currach when it rose slowly on the peaks of the waves. Each time that it had sunk out of sight again for a moment, my heart had squeezed dry with fear that it would never appear again. Now, because we were down on its own level, when we went forward to peer about for the currach, there was nothing to be seen but slate-grey waves edged with white. We looked back towards the quay and saw the people standing motionless, as they had done in the early part of the currach race when the boats had seemed to be in danger. I thought that if they had seen the Viking's currach sink, they would now be shouting and waving to us to come home. And if it sank, weighted as it was, it would never rise again in our lifetime.

Then Rooster, standing between us, called out suddenly:

"I'd swear I saw it there!"

We followed his pointing finger, but we could see nothing.

" 'Tis there again," said Rooster. He signalled to Lord who was at the helm to change his course a little to the east.

"It followed the current, sure enough. Now if we can get it before it's washed on to the reef, it will be safe."

Then we saw it ourselves. Now that we were close, it seemed to be moving faster. I could almost imagine that the ghost of the Viking was rowing it with invisible oars, so swiftly did it float on the current that was taking it to the reef.

Again Rooster signalled, and again Lord changed our course. Now we could see that they intended to sail in between the currach and the submerged end of the reef, so as to intercept it before it had gone too far.

My grandfather went clambering down to the stern.

"Mind the reef!" he shouted. He stopped when he saw Lord and Rooster exchange amused glances. "Who am I advising?" he said helplessly. " 'Tis a sign you're getting old when the young fellows are as well able to sail a boat as yourself."

"Wasn't it you that taught us, Granddad?" said Lord.

" 'Twas, faith," said the old man delightedly. "And well I did it."

I do not like to think what would have been the end of this story if the wind had not shifted just then. We were doing a foolhardy and dangerous thing, even with experienced sailors aboard, to sail so close in on a rocky lee shore. On Barrinish, we battle with the sea every day of our lives, and none of us wants to give her the satisfaction of winning that battle. Until I felt the land wind turning us away from that wicked shore, I had horrid visions of joining the band of seal-men so

vividly described by Louan. I did not want to
spend an endless lifetime sitting on wet rocks
and lonely sands, singing unwillingly the
miserable old songs of the seal-men. Above
all, I did not want my ghost to haunt the
Singing Cave.

Even in the midst of such a storm, the
water over the end of the reef seemed almost
calm. This was because it was sucked about
in little smooth whirlpools, before driving in
towards the brown rocks in huge, tumbling,
roaring fountains of spray.

At a sign from Rooster, Lord brought the
boat around in a great sweep, so that it
crossed the calm patch, surely at the very
jaws of the reef. We ducked our heads as the
boom swung across. She heeled over, down to
the gunwale. The top of a long wave splashed
aboard her before she righted herself. There
came the currach, sailing swiftly, still propelled by an invisible power. Rooster stood by
the bows with the boathook. Tom and I lay
close behind him. Again Lord swung the helm,
so that we crossed the currach's bows. Rooster
stabbed with the boathook, and in the same
moment Tom and I leaned far over the side of
the hooker and had seized the currach.

It came quietly enough, though I should

not have been surprised if it had been twitched out of our hands by its outraged passenger. We picked the trailing tow-rope out of the water so that we had it like a dog on a lead.

"This is a good day's work," said Rooster exultantly.

Silently I looked down into the currach at the three boxes. The biggest one contained the Viking's bones. In one of the others the remains of his once-powerful boat were packed, and in the last were his sword and his heavy horned helmet, and the game at which he had gazed for a thousand years. Then I knew what we we must do.

"We're not taking him back to Barrinish," I said.

Rooster looked at me with pity.

"There aren't many things I wouldn't do for you, Pat," he said. "But we can't go in to Galway in weather like this. Once we'd leave the shelter of the islands, we wouldn't last ten minutes."

"We can go home to Barrinish," I said, "but we won't bring the Viking with us."

"Speak plain," said my grandfather.

"We'll bury him at sea," I said. "It would be more fitting than to have him kept in a museum, like something that never was a

man, with no company but people like Mr
Allen. 'Twould be more fitting for him to lie at
the bottom of the sea, with his boat and his
sword and his helmet."

"And his game?" my grandfather asked on
a quick, panting breath.

"I'd like to keep the game," I said, and I
was astonished at how weakly my words expressed my burning longing to own that little
piece of wood with its curved ivory figures.

" 'Twould be more fitting, sure enough,"
said the old man. "But I have never seen your
Viking. I never asked you to show him to me,
all the journey home from Kermanach. I have
a wish to see him once, before he goes to his
rest."

"How can that be done?" said Lord. "We
could never get even one of those boxes aboard
in a sea like this."

Before anyone could stop me, I had skipped
over the side and dropped down into the
currach. It rocked sharply, so that for a long
moment it looked as if I and my Viking might
be buried together. Above me, Tom and the
men looked down with terrified faces until
the currach steadied a little.

Slowly and carefully I knelt down and
opened the hasp of the biggest box and lifted

back the lid. There he lay, my old friend, and I felt as I gazed at him that I had known him all my life. Very carefully, I leaned across and opened the second box. I shuddered with fear of the hurrying sea, streaming past so close. The wind took the lid of the box out of my hand and dropped it with a crash. The game was on top of the other things. I lifted it as carefully as if it had been a nest of eggs. Tom leaned down and took it from my hands, and I watched him store it safely in the lee of the cabin.

I wish I could forget how I opened the last box and then dropped all the things, one by one, overboard into the sea. The pieces of the boat floated away, so that I wondered if some of them would yet be washed ashore. Everything else sank to the bottom immediately, there at the end of the shrieking reef, whose claws I knew would hold them for ever and ever. To this day I cannot tell if I did right. I only know that that was the hardest day's work I have ever done.

Rooster helped me up into the hooker at last. He and Lord brought the boat around and we began to tack towards the harbour. For a long time no one said anything about what I had done. At last my grandfather sighed heavily.

" 'Twas for the best, I suppose," he said. "What are we going to tell the people at home?"

"We must tell them the truth," I said. "That is their due. And we promised Patsy Ward that he could make a play of the whole story when it would be finished. When he does that, the whole of Connacht will know about it."

" 'Tis true for you," said my grandfather. "I'm thinking we won't have much peace from now on."

"Perhaps the people outside of Barrinish won't believe it ever happened," I said. "Do you remember that Mr Allen didn't believe in the game though you and I had both seen it?"

"He believed in it, all right," said my grandfather sadly. "That was his whole trouble."

Now the people had seen that we were on our way home at last. Their cheers and calls were carried to us on the sweeping wind. As we came closer, they climbed down off the high wall and crowded on to the quay, so that it seemed as if every soul on the island was gathered there waiting for us.

Then I saw a solitary figure running along

the strand from the direction of the sports field. It was Johnny Gill, still carrying his sack. When we reached the quay, he had already forced his way to the front of the crowd so that he was in momently danger of being pushed into the water.

"Ye spoiled the sack race," he said accusingly, the moment we had our hooker by the steps. "Ye drew the crowds away from the field. 'Tis a disgrace and a scandal in this parish to have sports without no sack race. I'll report ye to the Bishop, so I will. I'll tell Máirtín Mór in Galway on ye, so I will, and he'll tell the highest in the land."

"Easy on, Johnny," said Lord soothingly. "The sports are not over yet." He raised his voice and trumpeted: "And the next event is the sack race. 'Twill be a match worth seeing, our own Johnny Gill and Michael Bán of Brosna. Up to the field, everyone! Come on, let ye, before the rain starts. Up to the field!"

And in a few minutes he had everyone streaming off the quay, joking and laughing and encouraging Johnny to uphold the honour of Barrinish. We had to go too, of course, for Johnny would have been mortally offended if we had not. Patsy Ward brought me to his caravan first and we gave the game to Mrs

Ward to mind. Her exclamations of astonishment at its strange beauty made me savour in advance the pleasure of showing it off to all our neighbours that very evening. Now at last I knew for certain that I was not going to be deprived of that pleasure.

Though I saw the sack race through a kind of fog, I know every stratagem by which Johnny contrived to reach the winning-post first, because Johnny himself has told me of them so often. He said that there was nothing in the rules to prevent him from shouting insults at his adversary, for instance, so that he would be delayed by spasms of fury. And he had hoped that no one saw him shouldering Michael Bán so that he fell only a yard from the end. But they did see, of course, and the race was declared a draw. Johnny was consoled at last by a promise that there would be another sack race next year.

" 'Twill have to do, I suppose," he said. "And I'll ask Mr Allen if I can keep the sack. Though I didn't do the job he gave me, he might let me keep the sack."

"What job was that, Johnny?" asked Lord gently.

"I refused to do it. I did, faith, for you were always fair to me, Lordeen. That's what I told him, too. I said to him, there's many a one that I'd drive their cattle, if they had them, but I won't drive Lord's cattle, not if you gave me a sack as big as the island and Michael Bán tied up inside in it."

Michael Bán, standing by, gave a growl of justifiable anger at this. Johnny turned a majestic eye on him.

"And that would be a tempting thing to be offered, so it would. Mr Allen thought I was soft enough to drive the cattle without knowing what I was doing, but I'm not as soft as all that. And I'll tell you another thing: I'd rather be soft than hard, any day of the week."

The rain began in earnest then, and the sports were over for the day. In high good humour, the men escorted Johnny and Michael Bán up the field and into Bartley Connor's public house, where a barrel was tapped. Bartley took Lord and my grandfather aside and told them that the tailor had just left to go home, in a miserable state of remorse over the help that he had given to Mr Allen.

"He got carried away," said Bartley, who knew a great deal about human nature because of his trade. "He has nothing against Lord. He hardly knew that Lord's cattle were in danger, he was so mad to do a bad turn to you, Mick."

"To me!" My grandfather was astonished. "Tailor and I were the best of friends, always."

Bartley lowered his voice still further, and turned his shoulder towards the men who were nearest so that they could not hear.

"That's only on the outside, Mick," he said. "Inside he's burning like a limekiln with jealousy."

"Jealous! Of me! He has a much finer life than I have!"

"Quiet, for the love of Mike, quiet. 'Tis the visiting house he wants. 'Twould draw a tear from a stepmother to hear him talk of the lonesome feel that comes over him of an evening, when he knows the men are all gathered into your house, and he must sit at home stitching away at the clothes, without so much as a cat to throw a word to. He knows the men only come down to him when you're not at home. And he says, of all men in the island that longs for news, himself must come first, for he doesn't go to the fields, nor to the bog, nor on the sea, nor to any of the places where the news is going around, except maybe on the day of the sports. I'll tell you true, Mick, I was heart sorry for him."

My grandfather was very much struck with

this. He had never had the smallest suspicion of it. All through that evening's celebrations he was very quiet. When the time came to go to Patsy's circus, everyone moved down to the tent which was like a little island of dim light in the surrounding blackness. I saw my grandfather looking about him anxiously, and presently he went across to talk to Lord. Then the two of them left the tent.

I was so engrossed in the tricks of Patsy's ponies that I took small notice of this. I know it is hard to ask anyone to believe it, but Patsy had those ponies trained to sit down on boxes, like Christians, and cross their legs. Tom and I swore that we would get to work on our young horse, the next fine day, and make him do the same.

"But we'll have to ask Patsy how you begin," I said, foreseeing already that it would not be plain sailing.

Then, just as Patsy's eldest son came out to announce the start of the evening's play, Lord and my grandfather were back. And they had the tailor between them. They came over to our bench.

"Move in, boys," said my grandfather easily. "We just went up for Tailor, fearing he'd miss the play."

The people around nodded approvingly. Not a soul would have given him an unfriendly look, seeing the company he was in. He kept his eyes down until the play began, and then gradually lifted them as the scene before us all became more and more interesting. By the time the evening was over, Tailor was one of ourselves again.

That was the beginning of a firm friendship between him and my grandfather. They had a great deal in common, and they soon found that by spending a lot of time in each other's company, neither of them missed any of the fun of the island. They came to a splendid arrangement about the question of who was to have the visiting house. Not a word was said, but on the evenings we had visitors, as soon as it came to nine o'clock the latch would be lifted and the tailor would come in with his evening's work in a bundle under his arm. Then he would climb on to our kitchen table and get on with it there. On several evenings of the week, at half-past eight my grandfather would stand up and stretch himself and say:

"How about going down to Tailor's place tonight? 'Twill be a change of scene for me, at least."

And we would all solemnly agree, and get

up and walk down the road to the tailor's house. He always looked up suddenly as if he were surprised to see us.

"Come in, men, come in," he would say in his soft voice. "I hope I have chairs enough for all."

I had a personal reason for being glad of this. It was soon clear that my grandfather intended eventually to bequeath the visiting house to the tailor instead of to me. This took a great load off my mind as well as off his, for I was never made to be a host. I was no good for starting a dance, or an argument, nor being bold enough, I suppose. And the tailor, for all his quiet ways, was a natural leader.

Besides, I was soon too busy. When Mr Allen recovered enough to leave Lord's house and go home, he came one day to visit us. He sat for a long time without speaking, and at last he said that he had come to offer to educate me. After a cold discussion, my grandfather agreed. Soon I was spending a great deal of time with Mr Allen, listening to him talk and reading his books. In time I became fond of him again. I learned many things from him, but he was always slow to mention the early history of Ireland, lest the ghost of a Viking might appear in the air between us and unbalance our friendship. Until I noticed this, I had almost begun to believe that he had forgotten about the Singing Cave, for he never again spoke of it.

If Sarah had still been his housekeeper, I doubt if I could have brought myself to visit him so often. But Sarah was never seen in Barrinish again. She went to live in Galway, saying that it was more convenient for her sailor husband between voyages. He was a quiet, decent man, but I never heard that the remaining six Seáns of Le Clé and their wives regretted their departure.

Mr Allen and my grandfather avoided each other. I suppose that because they belonged to the same generation, the hurt had gone too deep with them ever to be healed.

Big Dan came back to Barrinish a few weeks later, bringing Rooster's currach with him. He was very polite to everyone, and he had never paid better prices for our lobsters. No one spoke to him of the Singing Cave, and he did not stay on the island a moment longer than was necessary.

Louan came often in a Breton sardine-boat, which was a great curiosity for us. His son, Ronàn, came with him, and he soon became a close friend of mine.

As for the game of wolves, it was the delight of the whole of Barrinish before a month was up. We made our own rules, and some of the men became very skilled at the game. Rooster was champion of the island for several years, until Corny Lynch seized the title from him.

We never show the game to an outsider unless he is a man we can trust, a man who is well known to us all for many a year. When my grandson becomes its owner, I hope he will be as careful.

By the same author:

The Seekers

"A smoothly-written historical novel…the story provides a convincing, engaging portrait of the period."

Publishers Weekly

Children's
POOLBEG

Children's
POOLBEG

To get regular
information about
our books and authors join

THE POOLBEG
BOOK CLUB

To become a member of
THE POOLBEG BOOK CLUB
Write to Anne O'Reilly,
The Poolbeg Book Club,
Knocksedan House,
Swords, Co. Dublin.
Please write clearly and make sure to include
all the following details: Name, full address,
date of birth, school.

Children's Poolbeg Books

Author	Title	ISBN	Price
Banville Vincent	Hennessy	1 85371 132 2	£3.99
Beckett Mary	Orla was Six	1 85371 047 4	£2.99
Beckett Mary	Orla at School	1 85371 157 8	£2.99
Comyns Michael	The Trouble with Marrows	1 85371 117 9	£2.99
Considine June	When the Luvenders came to Merrick Town	1 85371 055 5	£4.50
Considine June	Luvenders at the Old Mill	1 85371 115 2	£4.50
Considine June	Island of Luvenders	1 85371 149 7	£4.50
Corcoran Clodagh ed.	Baker's Dozen	1 85371 050 4	£3.50
Corcoran Clodagh ed.	Discoveries	1 85371 019 9	£4.99
Cruickshank Margrit	SKUNK and the Ozone Conspiracy	1 85371 067 9	£3.99
Cruickshank Margrit	SKUNK and the Splitting Earth	1 85371 119 5	£3.99
Daly Ita	Candy on the DART	1 85371 057 1	£2.99
Daly Ita	Candy and Sharon Olé	1 85371 159 4	£3.50
Dillon Eilís	The Seekers	1 85371 152 7	£3.50
Dillon Eilís	The Singing Cave	1 85371 153 5	£3.99
Duffy Robert	Children's Quizbook No.1	1 85371 020 2	£2.99
Duffy Robert	Children's Quizbook No.2	1 85371 052 0	£2.99
Duffy Robert	Children's Quizbook No.3	1 85371 099 7	£2.99
Duffy Robert	The Euroquiz Book	1 85371 151 9	£3.50
Ellis Brendan	Santa and the King of Starless Nights	1 85371 114 4	£2.99
Henning Ann	The Connemara Whirlwind	1 85371 079 2	£3.99
Henning Ann	The Connemara Stallion	1 85371 158 6	£3.99
Hickey Tony	Blanketland	1 85371 043 1	£2.99
Hickey Tony	Foodland	1 85371 075 X	£2.99
Hickey Tony	Legendland	1 85371 122 5	£3.50
Hickey Tony	Where is Joe?	1 85371 045 8	£3.99
Hickey Tony	Joe in the Middle	1 85371 021 0	£3.99
Hickey Tony	Joe on Holiday	1 85371 145 4	£3.50
Hickey Tony	Spike & the Professor	1 85371 039 3	£2.99
Hickey Tony	Spike and the Professor and Doreen at the Races	1 85371 089 X	£3.50
Hickey Tony	Spike, the Professor and Doreen in London	1 85371 130 6	£3.99
Kelly Eamon	The Bridge of Feathers	1 85371 053 9	£2.99
Lavin Mary	A Likely Story	1 85371 104 7	£2.99
Lynch Patricia	Brogeen and the Green Shoes	1 85371 051 2	£3.50
Lynch Patricia	Brogeen follows the Magic Tune	1 85371 022 9	£2.99
Lynch Patricia	Sally from Cork	1 85371 070 9	£3.99
Lynch Patricia	The Turfcutter's Donkey	1 85371 016 4	£3.99
MacMahon Bryan	Patsy-O	1 85371 036 9	£3.50
McCann Sean	Growing Things	1 85371 029 6	£2.99
McMahon Sean	The Poolbeg Book of Children's Verse	1 85371 080 6	£4.99
McMahon Sean	Shoes and Ships and Sealing Wax	1 85371 046 6	£2.99
McMahon Sean	The Light on Illancrone	1 85371 083 0	£3.50
McMahon Sean	The Three Seals	1 85371 148 9	£3.99
Mullen Michael	The Viking Princess	1 85371 015 6	£2.99
Mullen Michael	The Caravan	1 85371 074 1	£2.99
Mullen Michael	The Little Drummer Boy	1 85371 035 0	£2.99
Mullen Michael	The Long March	1 85371 109 8	£3.50
Mullen Michael	The Flight of the Earls	1 85371 146 2	£3.99
Ní Dhuibhne Eilís	The Uncommon Cormorant	1 85371 111 X	£2.99

Author	Title	ISBN	Price
Ní Dhuibhne Eilís	Hugo and the Sunshine Girl	1 85371 160 8	£3.50
Ó hEithir Breandán	An Nollaig Thiar	1 85371 044 X	£2.99
Ó Faoláin Eileen	The Little Black Hen	1 85371 049 0	£2.99
Ó Faoláin Eileen	Children of the Salmon	1 85371 003 2	£3.99
Ó Faoláin Eileen	Irish Sagas and Folk Tales	0 90516 971 9	£3.95
Quarton Marjorie	The Cow Watched the Battle	1 85371 084 9	£2.99
Quarton Marjorie	The Other Side of the Island	1 85371 161 6	£3.50
Quinn John	The Summer of Lily and Esme	1 85371 162 4	£3.99
Ross Gaby	Damien the Dragon	1 85371 078 4	£2.99
Schulman Anne	Children's Book of Puzzles	1 85371 133 0	£3.99
Snell Gordon	Cruncher Sparrow High Flier	1 85371 100 4	£2.99
Snell Gordon	Cruncher Sparrow's Flying School	1 85371 163 2	£2.99
Stanley-Higel Mary	Poolbeg Book of Children's Crosswords 1	1 85371 098 9	£2.99
Stanley-Higel Mary	Poolbeg Book of Children's Crosswords 2	1 85371 150 0	£3.50
Swift Carolyn	Bugsy Goes to Cork	1 85371 071 7	£3.50
Swift Carolyn	Bugsy Goes to Limerick	1 85371 014 8	£3.50
Swift Carolyn	Bugsy Goes to Galway	1 85371 147 0	£3.99
Swift Carolyn	Irish Myths and Tales	1 85371 103 9	£2.99
Swift Carolyn	Robbers on TV	1 85371 033 4	£2.99
Swift Carolyn	Robbers on the Streets	1 85371 113 6	£3.50
Traynor Shaun	A Little Man in England	1 85371 032 6	£2.99
Traynor Shaun	Hugo O'Huge	1 85371 048 2	£2.99
Traynor Shaun	The Giants' Olympics	1 85371 088 1	£2.99
Traynor Shaun	The Lost City of Belfast	1 85371 164 0	£3.50
	The Ultimate Children's Joke Book	1 85371 168 3	£2.99

While every effort is made to keep prices low, it is sometimes necessary to increase prices at short notice. Poolbeg Press Ltd reserves the right to show new retail prices on covers which may differ from those previously advertised in the text or elsewhere.

All Poolbeg books are available at your bookshop or newsagent or can be ordered from:

Poolbeg Press Knocksedan House
Forrest Great Swords Co Dublin
Tel: 01 407433 Fax: 01 403753

Please send a cheque or postal order (no currency) made payable to Poolbeg Press Ltd.

Allow 80p for postage for the first book, plus 50p for each additional book ordered.